J.W. TAN

# AND IN THIS STATE
# SHE GALLOPS

ISBN 9781790439881

http://jaydoubleutan.wixsite.com/apparentlyrealwriter

To my beta readers.

# Contents

## LOVERS' BRAINS

Held in the arms of a tall pine, the knobbly-limbed sprite watches the woodland. From somewhere not too far away, the wind brings It a song. It is a silly song, such as a child might sing to pass the time and lift the silence. But the voice is not that of a child. Closer and closer it comes, until the pine sprite can see her approaching below It, walking as surely as if she were on a path.

Her hair is bright red, vermillion red, and she carries a large red bag over one bare shoulder. Pine watches her skip between the trees, finding small flowers in the undergrowth and plucking them for her growing posy. Pine hops from branch to branch to follow her on her way, wondering where she is going, wandering alone away from the path in the woods.

'There you are!' she cries all of a sudden.

Pine has been so fixated on the shine of the sun on her glossy locks that It has not noticed the other person approaching. The young woman throws her bag aside and flings herself into the arms of the man to cover him with her crimson lips. Pine finds her mouth curious. Nothing about the man is lost when she finally releases him, pats down her hair, straightens out her dress. She pounced on him with hunger, and yet has devoured nothing of him.

'What have you got in there?' the young man asks, picking up her bag to hand back to her and feeling the weight of it.

'Just a little something for Granny and Gramps,' she says, and pulls out a large tin. She opens the lid to reveal sweet round buns, takes two and says with a cheeky wink, 'No harm in us having a couple.'

Pine watches the couple settle down against the trunk of Its tree and nibble their treats. It watches the woman snuggle closer and say,

'No harm in us being a little late, either.'

Pine has seen this sort of thing before, and though It finds it fascinating in a certain way, It can think of something that will entertain It more. It drops silently from Its tree and dances through the undergrowth, here and there, back and forth, searching.

It picks up a fir cone, but the weight is not enough.

It sees a fallen nest, but all the eggs are broken.

It finds mushrooms, but they are wide and flat.

Finally, It finds several smooth, round stones. It collects them in Its arms and takes them up into the branches of the tree above the distracted couple. With one open hand It reaches out over the spot where the cake tin lies, and the other hand It holds open above the pile of stones. It smiles Its jagged smile, and the buns are in the branches where It sits. With another silent jump It lands by the couple and puts the lid back on the tin.

The red-haired woman and her companion do not notice anything crawl closer to them along the forest floor, do not notice the sharp twig of a finger dragged quickly along the bottom of her foot, over the small hard mound of his ankle bone. There is no space in their minds for another.

Bored with their repetitive motion, Pine leaves the couple, following in the direction the woman had been heading. It finds a little clearing in the woods, a little pond, a little house. On the steps sits a little old man, and out of the window leans a little old woman. So quiet, so peaceful. Pine steps out of the shadows, a haze of glamour about It, and raises a hand in greeting to the man.

'How can I help you, young man? Are you lost?'

Pine says nothing, simply stretches Its lips as It moves closer, and when It is within striking distance swipes Its finger over the deep furrows of the man's forehead. The man crumples. Pine scoops him up in Its arms, takes him into the cottage's bedroom and lays him out on the bed. It tucks him up under the floral quilt and strokes his thin white hair with a near perfect imitation of care.

The woman is still as the needles that carpet the earth outside, her back now to the window and her eyes wide with fear. A little trickier, this one. Pine marks her cheek, lets her fall into Its arms, lowers her gently to the floor. A fire burns in the grate, so It takes the warmth and comfort, the protection and strength, and weaves a cloak, for It likes the clouds today and does not mean the old woman harm.

It unpicks her seams with one fingernail and slips into her skin. The rest of her It wraps in the cloak and hides in the wardrobe. As long as the wind stays absent, It will stitch her back together before It leaves.

*

Not until the sun has begun to bleed across the horizon do the woman and her man reach her grandparents' cottage, and neither of them have any inkling that something might be wrong. Smoke curls from the chimney, the smell of something hot and filling drifts from the window, the sound of Granny's humming reaches their ears.

'Granny! Gramps!' the woman calls, and she pushes open the door and kicks off her shoes. 'Sorry I'm late. I came half way here and realised I'd left your present at home!'

Granny turns away from the oven, grinning widely.

'Don't worry, my dear. You're here now. I'm afraid Gramps is ill. Pop your head round the door and see if he's awake. I'm sure he'd like to say hello.'

While the young woman slips into the bedroom, Granny turns her teeth on the young man standing awkwardly in the doorway.

'Hello,' he says. 'Pleasure to meet you. I've heard a lot about you, of course.'

He seems unsure of his body, shuffling from foot to foot, half-raising an arm, then holding his hand out for a formal shake. Granny laughs, takes his head in both hands and pulls him down to her level to smack a loud kiss onto each cheek.

'Welcome to the family, dear.'

'Thanks, Mrs –'

'None of that nonsense. I'm your Granny.'

The woman returns, shaking her head, a smile on her lips.

'Typical Gramps,' she says, setting her bag down on the table. 'Dead to the world. What's he got? Man 'flu?' She chuckles and pulls the tin out of her bag. 'This is what I nearly forgot.'

With a flourish, she opens the tin to reveal the stones inside. Granny claps her hands.

'Ooh, don't they look lovely!' She casts a sly half glance at each of them, to be sure the illusion is holding. 'It must be time for tea.'

She bustles about filling the kettle, fetching dainty little plates and pouring milk from the bottle into a small china jug.

The two young ones sit together on the small settee, while Granny sinks into her favourite armchair. She pours the tea and hands them each a rock on a plate. As she lifts her own to her mouth, she swaps it for one of the fresh buns and bites down into the sticky sweetness.

'My, my,' she says, licking her chops. 'You've turned into quite the little baker.'

The woman and her man each chomp down, scattering pearly white fragments to the floor. Granny watches until she has finished hers, then briefly lifts the glamour. With sudden cries of pain, the pair spit crumbling enamel, turn to each other, mouths foaming crimson and left with only shattered stumps. Then the veil is brought back down, and they smile and each take a sip of tea.

There is some talk after that, talk of small, silly things, of the man and his family, of the woman as a girl, and other such matters as one might talk of when introducing a sweetheart to a grandmother. Then the woman sighs happily and settles herself on the arm of Granny's chair, a hand on her shoulder and a cheek against her head.

'Will you do my hair, Granny? Like you used to?'

'Of course, my dear,' says Granny. 'You sit down there by my feet, and I shall pamper you to your delight.'

So the woman sits, and Granny begins to comb her long red hair, to twist and plait it between her fingers, all the while saying to the man things like,

'Oh, as a girl she'd have me comb her hair for hours.'

And,

'I do hope I live long enough to play with the hair of my great-grandchildren.'

And all the while he doesn't notice that she is pulling strand after strand out of the woman's scalp and carefully planting it in her shoulders until she has such a coat of fur growing there that she might be wearing a stole.

For one moment the man is allowed to see, and the horror in his eyes makes Granny's grin widen. So many little tricks flitting around in the air, just waiting to be plucked. So many oddities that could come to pass. What now?

'I have a little something for you, my dear,' Granny says to her new grandson, and she briefly disappears into the bedroom. What she fetches back with her appears to the couple to be a pair of heavy walking boots.

The woman gasps when she sees them.

'I didn't know you kept them, Granny.'

'My son used to go out hiking in these woods for days,' Granny explains.

'He took me with him, when I was a girl,' says the woman. 'We'd walk all day, and camp out wherever we ended up. He'd take me out when I got home from school at the end of the week, and we'd spend the whole weekend out there.'

Granny pats the woman's hand, for her eyes are shining with tears.

'I thought perhaps the two of you might like to keep those memories alive. They are good, solid boots. Lucky boots, if you believe in such a thing.' Her grin stretches again. She holds the boots out to the young man. 'Try them on, my dear.'

The young man places his left foot in the left boot, ties the laces tight and wiggles his toes around.

'A good fit,' he says. 'Very comfy.'

He takes the other from Granny, and sticks his right foot into the iron jaws of the trap.

'A fine pair of boots indeed,' he says, looking down at his booted foot and his mutilated foot. The teeth bite into him from ankle to knee, crunching right down to the bone.

Out in the woods an owl hoots, and Pine decides to stop. With a strand of Its own hair, pulled taut like a cheese wire, It slices off the man's leg. It clamps a hand over the stump to close the wound and lifts Its glamour. Then It strips off Granny's skin, takes it to the rest of her body in the cupboard, and sets about sewing it on again.

In the living room of the cottage, screams build up, die down, are drowned under a wave of sobs, and all while Pine stitches such neat seams that Granny will never notice when she wakes up. It tucks the old woman up in bed next to her husband and goes back to the young ones, eager to see the destruction before It moves on. The man crippled for life, the woman covered in beastly hair, both toothless before their time. It wants them to crumble, to run in revulsion from each other, to wander the world alone in their new oddball forms. The idea tickles It.

The two sit side by side on the floor, hands clasped over hands, cheek against cheek, all loud pain and sorrow exhausted.

'What empty gums we have,' says the young man.

'It would have happened one day, when we grew frail and old together.'

'Then all the better to bind us together, my sweetheart.'

'You chose a pretty sweetheart. What of all this horrid hair?'

The man picks up Granny's comb and begins to comb her new locks until they shine brighter even than they had when they cascaded from her head in the sunlight.

'What fine fur wings you have, my angel. All the better to fly us into the sunset.'

The woman laughs and shimmies her freshly decorated shoulders.

'And you,' says her man. 'You chose a sweetheart with a full body. What of this useless stump?'

The woman smiles slyly and kisses his sad lips until they join her.

'What fine imbalance you have, my love. All the better to help you kneel before me.'

And with fine red hair pulled from her shoulders, she plaits a pair of rings.

Pine watches the creatures. Disappointment flares briefly, and is extinguished with indifference.

Outside, the wind changes, and the knobbly-limbed sprite retreats to the embrace of Its favourite tree.

# DRAWN

Selene remembers nothing before the pain. She knows that she cannot walk, and she knows there is blood on her face, and she knows that she does not know where she is. The moon has set and her eyes sting in the dim light of the dawn sun. She tries to rise up from the earth, but her arms tremble beneath her weight and she falls again, face down in the dirt.

Something must have triggered this, she tells herself. This cannot be all life has been, will be, is. Her head hurts, but she searches it for clues.

All she finds is a vague sense that something has changed her, and from what she does not know.

The sun climbs, and the ache in her head turns to a heavy beating. She reaches out her arms again and pulls her body along the ground, just a little, just to prove she is not stuck. Nothing around her is familiar. Nothing tells her which way to go. Nothing reminds her of anything.

There are large leaves around her. It takes much effort and much time, but she manages to lift herself into a sitting position and wrap a leaf around her bleeding head. Upright now and more alert, she turns her head, slowly, to learn her new environment.

The leaves have fallen from large ferns, taller than she would be if she were standing, that crowd around her and leave little ground visible. Skinny trunks protrude from their tops, stretching high into the sky and bursting into balls of green far above. Everything feels a little damp, as though there has been rain recently. She can smell the moisture in the earth and leaves, and sees glistening, wiggling things in the undergrowth.

It has been hours now since she woke, and she stretches her legs in front of her and sees that they are steady. With the help of a trunk, she pulls herself to her full height and stands, for the first time, on her two feet.

She is wearing no clothes, and she never remembers doing so, but she is aware that others do and that she should.

Since nothing helps her decide with reason where to go, she closes her eyes, spins, and points.

The mud squeezing through her toes is pleasant.

The occasional drip from a leaf above to her face below is cooling.

The bird song is comforting, and makes her think that something around her used to make pretty sounds, before this here and now that she cannot quite grasp.

A rustling sound nearby does not startle her. She is curious to know who else, what else, is around her now, so she turns towards it.

There is someone else, lying in the ground as she had been, with blood on his arms. He moans and shields his eyes. He too has no clothes and looks in pain.

Selene wants him to be near her. She pulls, not with her body but with her mind, and he stretches his arms towards her and drags himself across the ground.

'Agilulf,' she says.

'Who..?' he chokes, but his words turn to groan as his head falls.

Selene bends down to the broken man, hooks her arms under his and hauls him up. He is skinny and hairy and bigger than her. She is soft and round, while he is all sharp angles. He is the colour of the soil, while she matches the white petals of the small flowers growing by her feet.

'Which way?' she asks him, and he manages to lift a hand and show her.

He stumbles with every step, but her firm hand on his chest and her arm around his back keep him upright and moving.

By the time they near the wooden hut, the sun is high and Selene has to close her lids against it. Without her sight, she picks her way through the world with her ears and nose, and finally takes Agilulf over the threshold of his home.

She finds cloth to bind his wounds, but sees that the blood comes from nowhere. His body aches, and he can hardly move, but his flesh has not been cut.

She tends to her own wound instead, then makes a small fire outside the hut on which to heat a pail of water so that Agilulf may bathe his arms.

He sleeps awhile, and so does she for she finds the sun too bright to let her wander around outside. When they wake it is dusk, and Selene sits on the step by the door and looks up into the sky. Stars begin to emerge, and she fancies she can hear them singing to her. She watches the ink spill of the night spread until every trace of daytime blue has been blotted out.

Agilulf comes to sit with her.

'How do you know my name?' he asks.

Selene shrugs her shoulders, for she does not know. She saw him, and she knew him, and she wanted to pull him closer, and that is all she knows.

'Who are you?' he asks.

'Selene,' she says, though she is not sure if she was Selene before, or if she is only Selene now.

'Are you cold?'

She shakes her head.

Agilulf has not dressed himself, either, but both are content to sit as they are, alone in the forest with nobody to tell them to do otherwise.

Agilulf roams the sky with his eyes, and his thick brows draw together. He stands, looks behind them over the roof of the hut, then sits back down beside Selene.

'So dark,' he mutters to himself.

'New moon,' says Selene.

'Impossible,' says Agilulf. 'She was full last night.'

'Are you sure?'

Agilulf nods fiercely.

'Maybe you misremember,' says Selene, and the thought makes her smile, for of course she remembers or misremembers nothing at all.

'I cannot misremember,' he says. His forehead tightens and from his eye falls a droplet, like those the leaves dripped on Selene in the morning. It reflects the starlight, and is followed by another, and another, until his face is covered like the night sky.

'She calls me when she is full,' he says, 'and I cannot resist her. She pulls at my flesh, at my blood, at my heart. She changes me in terrible ways.'

Selene puts a gentle hand to his arm and feels him shiver.

'She sounds so cruel,' she says. 'Surely you are glad that she has gone.'

Agilulf shakes his head, sending the wet little stars flying from his cheeks.

'She does not mean to hurt me,' he says. 'I know she doesn't. But she is far away, and she pulls me, and I cannot reach her. Every part of me wants to reach her, but no matter how I change I am never close enough, never high enough, never good enough.'

Something stirs in Selene's heart.

'Then it must pain her to see you in such torment,' she says. 'Perhaps she tries just as hard to reach down to you, to fall to you.'

Agilulf looks at the woman who glows before him, reflecting the light of the unseen sun with her pale skin. He touches her cheek with his palm, and she touches his with hers.

'Perhaps she has succeeded,' he says, and their lips meet.

'Perhaps,' says Selene, holding Agilulf closer than she ever dreamed possible, 'it is a new moon.'

## THIN OF SUBSTANCE

In the house where Odhrán lived was a presence he could not explain. Nobody else could feel a thing, but Odhrán knew that it had always been there. Sometimes, in an empty room, the blood in his veins would heat and pulse harder until he felt the throb in his wrists and neck and feet. Something would build in his chest, a pressure that made him want to scream aloud, yet for all his bellowing would never release. At the very point that he felt he could take this no more, a warmth would envelope his shoulders, his lips would tingle with a pleasant burn, and he would suddenly feel at perfect ease. His racing pulse would calm and his body would fill with liquid peace.

When Odhrán turned twenty-one, it was decided that he should soon be married, for his life was running away with him and he had yet nothing to show for it. Odhrán's mother and father were wealthy business owners with many good connections around the world, and so they began to make a list of all their wealthy acquaintances who had daughters of Odhrán's age.

'What kind of girl shall our son marry?' Odhrán's mother asked his father.

'The perfect wife is a wife like you, my dear,' said the father. 'And the boy certainly needs someone to keep him in line.'

The mother agreed.

'She must be quick-witted,' said she, 'and able to think strategically.'

'She must be able to convey compelling propositions at management level.'

'She must be able to develop and maintain relevant trusting relationships.'

'She must be able to deliver on key strategic goal plans.'

So the mother and the father wrote out their criteria and sent proposals to women all over the globe, asking them to apply as soon as possible if they were interested.

While his parents created the paperwork, Odhrán lay down on the floor of his bedroom, closed his eyes and whispered,

'Are you there?'

His fingertips began to thrum. His toes twitched. The black behind his eyelids grew red. His heart quickened and filled with that unidentifiable desire for something, for screams, for movement, for he could not say what.

Hot tears fell down his face and pooled in the hair above his ears.

*Shhhhhhhhhhhh. No tears.*

The warmth gathered at his shoulders and over his chest, and trickled down one arm.

'I don't want to.'

His nose began to clog, but he didn't want to move for fear of losing the presence.

*Trust me.*

'How can you stop it?'

A loud knock interrupted. The presence vanished before Odhrán had settled into calm.

He sat up, wiped his eyes, reached for a tissue and blew heavily. Then, knowing he could not wait long enough for the redness in his eyes to settle, he said,

'Come in.'

The father and mother pushed open the door and were both disgusted to see that the boy had been crying.

'What's wrong with you?' the mother demanded.

'Stop it. There is nothing in your life to cry about,' insisted the father.

Odhrán had learned years ago not to argue, so he bowed his head, mumbled an apology, and asked,

'Have you chosen someone yet?'

'We have a shortlist,' said the mother, and she waved a bundle of papers beneath his nose.

'We will go through the candidates together, and you can pick the ones you would like to interview.'

Odhrán had no interest in choosing his fiancé through paperwork, but the parents dragged him downstairs, brewed strong coffee, laid each application out on the table and began to take notes and discuss.

After many long hours, in which Odhrán clenched his toes and fists, tried to breathe quickly to increases his pulse, tried any number of subtle gestures to bring about the symptoms of the presence, it was decided that an initial three candidates would be invited individually to the house. Odhrán would have to interview each one, consider their worth, and then decide if he wished to view more applicants or make a final decision.

*

The first was Limbani. She was tall, taller than Odhrán, and wore a brightly coloured dress and shoes that added to her stature. Her handshake was firm and her eyes were kind. With both Limbani and Odhrán's parents present, they talked of the businesses they had been born into, of stock and profit and mergers and other appropriate things. Satisfied that the couple were well matched, the parents allowed them to take a stroll alone around the garden.

When they had gone, Odhrán's mother said to his father,

'We must test her ourselves, of course. Odhrán cannot be left to make this decision entirely based on his feelings.'

'No, that wouldn't do,' said the father. 'Who knows what reasons the boy would use! He can't make such an important decision on his own.'

Between them they decided to test Limbani's practical managerial skills by creating some disturbance in her stay.

'She must be able to complain and demand improvement,' said the mother, 'otherwise what kind of a workforce would she have below her?'

'But she must be able to criticise without offending,' said the father, 'or she would risk alienating partners and clients.'

The mother and father went to the room in which Limbani would be sleeping and placed under her mattress a rock to make her bed uncomfortable.

Meanwhile, in the garden, Odhrán laughed at Limbani's childhood tale of misadventure. Without their parents hearing their every word and recording their every move, the two were enjoying each other's company.

After a half hour of comfortable chatter, Odhrán felt comfortable enough to ask her,

'Do you enjoy being part of the family business?'

Limbani's shoulders shifted in a shrug that she hastily attempted to conceal as a roll of the neck, a wiggle of stiff joints.

'Of course,' she said, without meeting his eyes. 'We are both very lucky to have been born into such successful families. We have been blessed with positions of true privilege in our lives.'

'I know,' said Odhrán, growing bolder now that he was sure she was like him. 'I am very grateful to have been given so much. But do you ever feel that you want to do something of your own? Something that hasn't been handed to you?'

Limbani looked down into his eyes.

'That somebody else would give anything to have the position you have,' she said quietly. 'And that you do not deserve it because you do not want it. That you should be working towards your own success, not surfing the wave of your parents'.'

Without thinking, drawn by how exactly her words twinned his own thoughts, her grasped her hand in his.

'Exactly! But also that thinking such things – '

'Is so ungrateful, so self-centred, when we have such luck,' she finished for him, squeezing his hand back.

The pair held each other's gaze, eyes shining like two stars of the same constellation, hands joined and hearts beating with the same secret thoughts.

Then Limbani's eyes and hands dropped, and she stepped away from Odhrán.

'Sorry,' she said.

'For what?'

'I've enjoyed meeting you, Odhrán. I really have. We're a lot alike, you and I, but I'm not here for the right reasons. I applied because my parents wanted me to.'

Odhrán's friendly hand touched her shoulder.

'You're already in love with someone else, aren't you?'

She smiled at him, a smile of regret for him that held also the joy of her passion for another.

'It's okay,' said Odhrán, and he laughed with happiness for his newfound friend and relief for them both. 'I'm sure we're going to have a long friendship, Limbani. I don't really want a wife at all.'

The regret flew from her face, and side by side at the ornamental fountain Limbani and Odhrán laughed away their guilt at the deception their parents had led them into.

Late into the night Odhrán and Limbani shared words. They shared their dreads, the seemingly inevitable, the long gone mistakes and choices they would change in a heartbeat if they could.

When midnight had passed, just as they were thinking of retiring for the night, Odhrán found himself telling Limbani,

'There is something else I've never spoken of.'

'Oh?' she said. 'And what is that?'

He told her of the presence, of the feeling that overcame him whenever it was near, and of its protective promises.

'I don't know what it is, or why it is. There is so much I don't know, and yet...It is hard to explain the connection I have with it.'

Limbani's laugh was small and tired, but full of sleepy sincerity.

'I think it is easy,' she said.

Then she kissed Odhrán's cheek, bade him goodnight and went to her room, leaving Odhrán to wonder.

*

'How did you sleep?' the mother asked Limbani over breakfast.

Odhrán, of course, had no idea of the little plot his parents had hatched, but when Limbani had whispered to him of her lumpy mattress as they came down the stairs he had begun to suspect a test of some kind.

Before answering, Limbani met her friend's eye. He thought quickly, hoped for the best, made a very small shake of the head and ran a finger across his lips.

'Marvellously,' said Limbani. 'You have been wonderful hosts, I must say. Everything has been perfect.'

Odhrán watched his parents share a brief disapproving glance and smiled. He nodded his thanks to Limbani.

A great fuss was made that morning over farewells and well-wishes for the journey and thanks for the hospitality. Limbani rolled her eyes at Odhrán while the parents were distracted and slipped him a card with her details, her own personal card to counter the business ones their parents exchanged. They promised in whispers that their friendship would not end, wished each other the strength to follow their dreams, and Odhrán said,

'I hope one day you will marry your love.'

'And you,' she said with a wink, then she turned her eyes to empty space and wished a silent farewell to the presence she could not feel.

*

The second was Delilah. She was small and dainty and wrapped up in white furs. As soon as the door was opened to her, she smiled widely and blinked her long lashes at Odhrán.

'Goodness, you must be hot blooded to put up with this cold,' she said. 'Perhaps we could turn the heating up just a teensy bit while I'm here. I can be delicate. Though make no mistake, I am ruthless in the business word.'

She strode past him without being invited and flung open the nearest door.

'Is this the sitting room?' she asked, marching in and plonking herself down on a settee. 'Lovely. Is this how you'd like our house decorated, if we were married?'

Odhrán was rather taken aback by this woman's entrance, and had never really thought much about interior design.

'I don't know,' he answered honestly.

'Well, I'm sure we can find a middle ground between your tastes and mine.'

The parents gathered with them, and Delilah took the lead in explaining the ins and outs of her family's company.

Odhrán's concentration wandered. Trapped in this meeting that he felt no part of, he was lonely. The moments between each pump of his heart decreased. The pressure in his chest built, and built all the more now that he was not alone to speak to the presence.

The feeling mounted to an unbearable height, the height that made him want to run yelling through the world until he had no more breath, to get rid of whatever this great weight was.

He let out a small cry.

The others stopped dead and looked at him, his parents embarrassed, the rest confused.

'Excuse me,' he said, hiding his face. 'I don't feel quite myself.'

He fled the room, tears cascading as he did. He ran to the kitchen, turned on the tap with shaking hands and splashed himself with water.

'Are you here?' he gulped through his tears.

*I'm here.*

'What is this?'

*What is what?*

'This…in my chest. It hurts. Am I ill?' A terrible thought occurred then to Odhrán, something he had never considered before. 'Are you making me sick?'

The warmth surrounded him, evaporated his tears, calmed his thumping veins.

*I have done nothing to you. I never would.*

There was a visible haze now, like a cloud of steam or fog around him. It touched his skin where he felt the warmth, and it began to gather into a form.

'Are you okay?'

The presence vanished.

Delilah had followed him.

He nodded without turning to her, then filled a glass of water and drank, because it was something to do with his hands, and it was a normal thing to do when one was feeling unwell.

'I know you think I'm too brash, barging in here and trying to interfere with your business,' she said, settling herself on a stool at the breakfast bar and watching him severely. 'It's what everyone thinks of me.'

'I don't,' said Odhrán, and he realised as the words came that it was true. 'You might be brash, but it isn't *too* brash. It's just you, isn't it? I bet you're brilliant at work.'

Delilah brightened.

'Really? You're not put off?'

He shook his head.

'Lots of people are,' she said, and sighed heavily. 'Because I'm small and sweet looking, so that's how they want me to act.'

Odhrán shook his head. He knew that before Limbani he would not have said to anyone what he was about to say, but now he had seen beneath the surface of one perfect CV he wanted to see beneath the surface of everyone. Perhaps the innards of some matched the skin, perhaps many were mismatched.

'There's nothing wrong with disappointing people if what they want is for you to not be you.'

Delilah laughed loudly and reached out to give him a friendly slap on the shoulder.

'Very prettily put,' she said. 'Don't you worry. I've never been afraid of myself.'

They talked a while longer, both keeping an ear open for the intruding elders, until Odhrán said,

'I think you're probably the perfect candidate.'

'Perhaps I am, but you're not. You have no interest in your business, do you?'

Odhrán laughed.

'We are a pretty poor match,' he agreed.

'Yet they say opposites attract.'

'In that case, I hope a long friendship has been born.'

'Likewise.'

The next morning, Odhrán knew he had nothing to fear. Though his mother asked how Delilah had slept, and though she answered, firmly but with perfect tact, that there was room for improvement, Odhrán knew he would never be married to Delilah.

The satisfied look his parents exchanged only made him chuckle inwardly. When Delilah and her parents took their leave, she made a diplomatic farewell speech.

'I do wish you the very best luck in your search for a wife, Odhrán,' she said as she took his hand in hers. 'I do hope this friendship lasts, and that our two businesses can be of use to each other in the future.'

She handed his parents a business card, and him a personal one.

The mother and father were most excited when she left.

'An excellent candidate,' said the father.

'She's definitely the one to beat so far,' said the mother.

Odhrán couldn't hold back the giggle.

'You didn't notice, did you?' he said. 'She really must be wonderful in the corporate world.'

'What do you mean?' asked the father.

'You came out of this all feeling flattered and accomplished, but she rejected me.'

Odhrán left his parents in their incredulous recounting of Delilah's words, in their stunned realisation that their offer had been dismissed, and went to his bedroom. He lay down and closed his eyes.

*Open them.*

The presence had gathered before him into the shadow of a human form.

*

The third was Leto. Leto was a lie. The woman who arrived was not accompanied and she was not young. Her suit was well pressed and her

24

hair sprayed in place, and had she been the mother of an applicant Odhrán's father and mother may well have been impressed.

'We should still give her a chance,' said the mother.

'Age is only a number,' said the father. 'They may well get on.'

Odhrán did not want to give her a chance. She was twice his age, if not more, and he did not like the way she looked at him.

'I love a young man in my business,' she said to his parents, eyeing Odhrán from head to toe. 'So energetic, so bold, so virile.'

She told his parents how she had been born into a family of actors.

'Very hard working, but artsy types,' she said. 'I like things a little more grounded.'

Her business was her own. She had built it and she had earned it. The more she talked, the less her eyes lingered on Odhrán.

After some time, much longer than the meetings with his previous suitors, Odhrán's parents excused themselves and left Leto with the boy.

'I feel I owe you an apology,' she said as soon as they were alone.

Odhrán said nothing, for he was not sure what Leto was talking about.

'I am used to young men quite different from yourself. They are young in body, young in stamina, but have the mature minds of a mogul much more senior in years.'

She smiled at Odhrán, and this time her look was that of an aunt fondly regarding a nephew she was proud of.

'You have a young mind, off in the clouds, don't you, Odhrán?'

Odhrán shrugged awkwardly. She talked to him like a friendly teacher, kind but quite obviously above his level, and he could not speak to her as freely as to the younger women.

'Maybe,' was all he said.

'Definitely,' said Leto. 'So I apologise. The number is not important to me, but your mind is too young. I would never bed a man with an adolescent mind.'

Leto did not stay the night. She and Odhrán could not find his parents, to whom she wanted to make apologies and bid goodbye, so instead she gave him a message to pass on, her business card in case he ever wanted any advice, and a platonic cuddle because his face was full of concern.

'Don't worry, Odhrán. You will find a wife who suits you, I'm sure.'

Alone now, Odhrán did what he always did. He sat down on his bedroom floor, removed the smart jacket he had been wearing for the meeting, undid the top few buttons of his shirt, kicked off his polished black brogues. Before he had even lain down and begun to concentrate, a foggy figure appeared before him. He watched it, and his pulse raced. The little lump that had been sitting on his heart all day expanded, and his eyes grew hot with tears. The fog grew firmer, more substantial, more human with every pound of Odhrán's heart. The dark patches at its head formed into emerald eyes. Its lips turned full and dark, and raven tresses curled to its chin. Soon a young man stood before Odhrán, a honey-skinned, freckled man dressed in a simple linen shirt and trousers, his feet bare and his hair a tousled jumble.

'Might you have time to meet with one more candidate today?' he asked, and the voice was so familiar that Odhrán's heart overflowed.

'You can't be real,' he said. 'You've never been real like this.'

'Because you've never felt quite so much like this.'

'It can't be real!'

'Why can't it? Why can't I?'

Odhrán buried his damp face in his hands, wishing the vision would pass.

'Because I want it too much,' he cried. 'Because Limbani was right. It *is* easy to explain, and it hurts.'

He raised his tear strewn face to the figure before him, and the force of his feelings and the impossibility of his future punched him hard in the stomach.

'I am in love with a ghost.'

*

Late that night when Odhrán's father and mother arrived back home, for they had been walking in the gardens for hours to give Odhrán and Leto time to bond, they felt a presence that had not been there before.

'Odhrán?' called the father.

There was no reply, no boy coming into the hall to greet them, so they climbed the stairs to the first floor.

'Odhrán?' called the mother.

The presence they could feel came from the spare room, the one in which the women had been sleeping on the rock, so they opened the door and looked in.

Odhrán slept peacefully, curled up in the arms of a young man they had never seen before.

'Your actions are full of tricks instead of feelings,' said the young man, and he tossed the rock to them. It landed on the carpet with a dull thud.

'Who are you?' the mother demanded. 'I have not received your application.'

'You have not been offered an interview,' added the father

'Marriage is not business,' said the young man, his tender gaze on Odhrán's sleeping face. 'Love is not business. Your son is not your company.'

'Who are you?' the mother asked again.

'Just a presence in your house,' said the young man. 'Something you never noticed. Something to love Odhrán when no-one else cared to.'

Odhrán stirred. He nestled his head into the young man's chest, opened his eyes, smiled up at him. Then he noticed the father and the mother. He rubbed the weariness from his eyes, took strength from the presence by his side, and told them,

'I have made my decision.'

'Decision?' asked the father.

'About my marriage,' said Odhrán.

'That is not your decision to make alone,' said the mother. 'We need to discuss – '

'There is nothing to discuss,' said Odhrán, and it was the first time in his life that he had ever interrupted his mother. 'I am not going to marry any of the candidates. I am not going to marry my one candidate either. I am not going to live here with you anymore, and I am not going to work for you.'

'Where will you go, then?' asked the mother.

'What will you do?' asked the father.

*

Many months later, Odhrán stepped out of his flat and made his way down the hallway. Five doors down, he knocked. Limbani opened her door.

'Odhrán! Come in, come in. Who's your friend?'

'Salvator,' said Odhrán.

Limbani stared into the young man's green eyes.

'Salvator,' she whispered. 'I can see you.'

'And I you. It is nice to be able to talk to you, after all this time.'

When the light hit him in a certain way, one might almost think that Salvator did not look entirely solid. Once in a while his fingertips might

27

seem to allow objects through them, as though his hands were coloured steam. When he spoke, his voice might seem to disappear for a moment, like a radio with a weak signal.

Limbani brought steaming mugs of rooibos tea to her guests and led them through a pair of tall glass doors.

'Delilah wants to fly us out to hers next weekend,' she told them. 'She has found a new favourite haunt that she absolutely *must* show us.'

Sitting on Limbani's balcony in the sunshine, Odhrán stretched his arms out wide. Beneath his ribs he felt that his heart was full, so full that he could scream with joy. He stood, and with him stood his companions, stood together to look out over the hot city below them.

In one voice, Salvator, Limbani and Odhrán bellowed their bliss to the open sky.

## STRAIGHT ON KISSES DREAM

The baby was born with big brown eyes. He cried up at his mother while she whispered his name in his ear.

Close by, One waited in the shadows. It caught the name between Its crooked fingers and shaped it into something else. When the mother fell asleep, It scooped the baby up in Its arms and laid the new One gently to rest.

In the morning, the mother stroked her boy's head, kissed his nose, sang into his fresh little ears. He blinked his amber eyes and watched this curious creature fuss over him.

The One known as Aiden grew. He learnt the language of the funny, helpless creatures he lived with, but they seemed incapable of learning any of his. They thought he was a sweet little boy playing games when he spoke to the trees and the birds and the spiders and heard their news.

After fifteen years, on a whim, he left. He had no quarrel with his family, and there was no logic that could explain his decision. His choices were made from curiosity, or boredom, or because of which way the tide was pulling, or how the next sycamore landed.

Several things happened in the following years.

The clock at Durham Cathedral began to tick backwards, and the maintenance man sent to fix it was seen adding another six hands. He had a bruise or smudge of some kind on his neck.

Shortly afterwards, in a small village called Staindrop, seven different people, each with a strange mark on their face, decided on the same morning to paint their houses a shocking shade of pink.

At Darlington station, everybody in the vicinity one day swore that they had seen the back of a locomotive open into a wide mouth and gobble up the carriage behind it. The only people who claimed to have seen nothing were three members of staff, each of whom had a touch of green about their mouth.

And so such events continued, inexplicably and apparently unconnected, until the day the One known as Aiden turned twenty.

The tailor usually made formal suits, for weddings or funerals or a gentleman's daily needs, but the costume he made for Aiden was something else. It was exquisite. The forest green waistcoat locked his torso in a tight embrace, the high collar kissed his neck and whispered in his ear, the tails hung to his knees, floating gently in an unfelt breeze like the leaves of a weeping willow. A sliver of chestnut abdomen was visible between the last button of the waistcoat and the waistband of the trousers that clung to his legs like sodden petals to stone. His boots were high and soft as a carpet of moss, turned over just above the knee.

When the tailor named the final price, Aiden leant in to the curve of his jaw. His lips left behind a trace of green, and there was no more mention of money. Aiden would never return to this tailor, probably never to this city. His long boots took him far away, through a town, through a village, through a hamlet, into rich woodlands where he wove himself a crown of leaves and bark. He twisted dark creepers around his bare arms and stood by a clear pool to marvel at his own beauty.

Deeper into the woodlands, in the very centre, was a hidden marsh. To the eye it seemed a large green clearing, but the ground was treacherously soft and capable of swallowing up a human in scant minutes. The sounds of singing birds and scampering squirrels, the soft tread of game and the rustling of hidden things in dried leaves, were replaced in the marsh with deep croaks and humming and hisses. Drawn to these sounds, the One known as Aiden stepped more lightly than ever a human could and made his way to the centre of the marsh. He watched the damp, tender things, and the skinny flying things, and found the beauty in the subtle blend of their greens and browns, and in the sudden flashes of bright blues and reds of the things that darted in the air. As the light of the day faded, the clearing filled with gold dust as the fireflies emerged.

It was then that he heard the human sound, one of the many sad sounds they made when their faces leaked. Leaving no prints in the boggy ground, he skipped to the edge of the marsh and followed the sound through the trees, his eyes just as keen as they were with the help of the sun. A woman barely older than himself was lumbering through the woods, her feet heavy and loud, breaking branches and trampling low down dens. She could not see the way he could. He pressed his pearly green lips to her ear lobe, then silently called to a firefly. It hovered close to the woman, and she stopped quite suddenly to stare at it.

'It is quite safe,' he said, keeping his voice at the very edge of her mind. 'Follow its light.'

He called more, and they hovered in a winding trail towards the marsh. The woman took a few paces forwards, then stopped again.

'Let them guide you.'

Drawn to their warm glow, and encouraged by the voice that she did not realise she heard, the woman followed the trail of lights towards the hungry mire.

He kept close by her and examined her as she made her way to her own demise. For a human, her gait was almost graceful. Her feet were bare, and now that she had slowed her pace she crept through the earth on her toes, like the sneak-step of a dance. Her colouring put him in mind of a song thrush, speckled and brown. He wanted to touch her, to see if her skin was soft like feathers.

She was close to the edge of the trees now, close to taking her first step into the sinking mud.

Aiden waved a hand, and the fireflies shifted. They led her around the ring of trees, close to the edge on the honest land, and away towards the nearest hamlet. He followed her still, through the woods to the paths and back to the little houses. He tucked himself in the dark places and watched another young woman come running to embrace her, watched her taken safely inside, watched through the window as she was given hot soup and blankets.

Just beyond her hearing, he offered her his name.

*

'Why aren't we like them?' he asked the crooked-fingered One.

'A light and a dark, a mind and a heart, and never the twain shall meet.'

'They don't seem so different, some of the time. What if I kept one? I've always left them behind before.'

The Crooked One cackled.

'Behind or in front, in time or a place, an end is the only end in the end.'

Aiden sighed and pulled one of his curls gently out to full length, then let it spring back where it belonged.

'Can they like us?' he asked. 'Love us?' Then, 'Can *we* love at all?'

'A human kept or a human left, a fae's still a fae's still a fae.'

'What about me? I've met loads of them, all the time, every day. But of you, I've only ever met you. Am I one of you, or them?'

'Made in name or laugh or death, made isn't born, and born isn't made.'

When Aiden made no more questions, the Crooked One became small enough to step back onto Its bark taboggan, sang to Its nightingale and was carried off out the window into the dark.

A knock at the door brought the innkeeper's husband with a tray of bread and stew. Aiden took the tray and kissed the man's hand, whispered in his ear, and sent him on his way. The next morning, the innkeeper would find herself trying to explain to an array of furious guests why her husband had seen fit to offer up only a boiled leather boot for breakfast.

And yet the One known as Aiden felt nothing. No glee, no delight, not a chuckle escaped him. His mind focused only on the image of the woman, soup bowl in hands and blankets warming her, lips regaining a smile as she settled back into safety.

In his chest beat the imitation of a human heart, but if it was to have what it desired, he must become more than a likeness. If humans played with their kisses and whispers, it was simple games with each other, not games with the fabric of the world. No more, Aiden decided. At the looking glass that hung from the wall, he leaned in to kiss his own lips, sealing them.

*

Cara had never set foot into the woods before. When she had been sent as a girl to run errands in the nearest village, she had been told to go the long way around and had always obeyed. Now, the morning after her twenty-first birthday, still shivering at the memory of wandering alone the night before, she understood why. It had been so easy to lose her way, distracted by the bright flash of petals in the tangle of green. Her mother, a practical woman, had no time for such nonsense.

'Have you made a decision?' she asked as she and her daughter sat down to breakfast.

'About what, Mama?' asked Cara, her mind still on floating lights and barely heard whispers.

'About the Millstone boy.'

Cara sighed.

'Mama, he'll be away for another week. I don't have to answer until then.'

Her mother sighed and grumbled and bustled loudly about clearing the table. Cara waited patiently through this mild tantrum until her mother, as she always did in the end, snapped at her to make herself useful and gave her a list of errands.

On the little track to the farmer's house, she thought for a moment she saw the Millstone boy, and panic took her. Her answer was not ready. He was not supposed to be here.

But it wasn't him. She held a hand to her trembling heart and had to laugh at herself. This boy was a stranger, and all the stranger for his manner of dress. He wore all greens and browns, the colours of leaves and bark dappled with sunlight, and even from this distance she saw that his eyes shone amber.

'You're new to these parts, Sir,' she called. 'Have you lost your way, or are you intending to visit us?'

He smiled, and she saw now that he had coloured his lips to match his clothes. *What an eccentric young man*, she thought to herself, but the beauty of his smile drew her towards him regardless.

The young man lifted the crown of leaves from his head and bowed low, holding his hand out towards her. She hesitated, then placed her own in his and let him kiss the air a hair's breadth from her skin.

'My name is Cara,' she told him.

He locked his amber eyes on hers, put a hand to his chest and nodded, and Cara felt as though she had heard the words he had not said.

'It is a pleasure to meet you too, Sir. It is a funny thing, but you look somewhat like another young man I know.'

The eyes shone with curiosity.

'His name is Arnold Millstone. Perhaps he is a relation of yours? Is that why you have come here?'

He shook his head gently, and with the smallest wave of his hand gestured to Cara herself. She blushed and found herself laughing.

'But we have never met! You flatter me, Sir, but you cannot have come looking for a girl you do not know.'

And yet his eyes spoke no lie.

'Well then. If we are to be friends, I shall have to know your name. Can you write?'

He pointed to Cara, closed his hand into a loose fist, then touched it to his mouth and tapped his chest.

'Very well,' she said. 'I shall give you a name.'

She closed her eyes and cast around in her mind. Somewhere near the edge, something bit. She reeled it closer and closer until it fell off her tongue.

'Aiden.'

*

The Crooked One crept up to Aiden as he slept, curled up on a bale of hay in a barn near Cara's house.

'Nothing that's sealed cannot be opened. A kiss melts the seal of a kiss.'

Aiden kept his eyes closed and covered his ears with his palms. Not until morning did he move again, having slept no more, sure that the Crooked One had gone.

The longer he spent with Cara, the warmer his heart grew. He felt its rhythm change when he saw her, felt it fill at the sound of her voice, heard it sing at her touch on his arm.

One day, walking arm in arm through the fields in the sunlight, Cara said to him,

'I have an important decision to make.'

He asked with his eyes.

'Arnold Millstone,' she told him. 'He wants me to marry him. He returns home tomorrow, and I am to give him my answer.'

Aiden's eyes fell downwards. His smile melted in an instant. There was a sharp crack.

Cara glanced at the ground for the broken twig, still talking.

'He is kind, and hard-working, and has as much potential as anyone...'

Aiden's ears filled with the sound of another crack each time she spoke a good word about the Millstone boy. He let her talk, let her keep her hand on his arm, let her walk them both aimlessly through the grass. As the afternoon drew to a close, as she turned them back towards the hamlet, she asked,

'What shall I tell him?'

Aiden looked at the woman, this creature he could never be, her eyes alight with possible futures and her cheeks plump with a health and youth so much more temperamental than his own. He pulled the corners of his mouth up, with more effort than it had ever taken him before, and took both of her hands in his. He held her face with his steady amber eyes and nodded.

With a final crack, the remains of his imitation heart shattered.

*

On the Millstones' wedding day, One hid in the shadow of an oak, watching the dancing and the feasting and the never ending joy that filled the field by the little hamlet. Another joined him.

'No voice for the mind, no heart with to love, is empty and filled up with nothing inside.'

The Crooked One would have left Its companion there had a bird not landed above them and shaken a single acorn from the tree. The acorn fell at the feet of the Crooked One, so It reached out a crooked finger and sliced open Aiden's lips.

Aiden cried out, retched, coughed up the fragments of his heart and spat them onto the grass.

'Never again,' he declared.

And with his green, green lips, he set out once more to sprinkle the fabric of the world with his kisses.

## VAIN FANTASY

The was once a poor man who lived in a little wooden house with but one room. He had a wife, three sons, and three daughters, all of whom were very beautiful. The man loved his family, but no matter how hard he worked there never seemed to be enough money to provide for them all.

One day, his youngest and prettiest daughter came rushing inside crying,

'Father, Father! There is a great White Bear outside who will pay you handsomely if only you will let him take me away.'

The man went out to the White Bear.

'I am sorry, sir, but I would rather be a poor man to the end of my days than sell any one of my children.'

The White Bear bowed his head and said to the man,

'I have no desire to take a child from you, sir. I only wished to provide you with the means to build a better life for yourself and your family.'

The daughter was mightily disappointed, and spent every moment for a full week talking to her siblings about the clothes they could have worn, to her mother about all the rare and delightful food they could have eaten, and to her father about the sweet cottage they could have lived in. She fed her family such fanciful tales that they each began secretly to wish that her father had sent her away with the White Bear and made these dreams come true.

At the end of the week, the girl came running inside once more crying,

'Father, Father! The White Bear has returned! He has come once again to offer you gold if you will let him take me away.'

The man took his daughter in his arms.

'Don't worry, my darling,' he told the girl. 'I wouldn't give you up to a stranger. You have nothing to fear.'

'But Father,' said the girl, pulling away from the man, 'I would go willingly. Knowing that my family now have a life a thousand times better would keep my spirits up. And I'm sure the White Bear will be good company. He is well spoken and quite reasonable. Please, Father. Let me do this for you all.'

And though they knew they should be begging to keep their sister, the young girl's siblings all begged their father too.

'If she wants to go, let her!'

'Think of the food, Father!'

'Think of the clothes!'

'Think of the house!'

And so it was decided that the girl would go with the White Bear.

She wrapped a little food for the journey in her one spare dress, tucked the bundle under her cloak, and stepped outside to meet the bear. Her family wept to see her go, not knowing when she would be back, but she waved to them with a smile.

'I am yours now, White Bear.'

'Please do not be sad,' said the White Bear to the girl. 'A year and a day is not such a long time.'

The girl smiled and climbed onto his back.

'But for ever is, my darling.'

She felt the White Bear shiver.

Together they travelled through the wind and snow until they came to a small cave mouth at the base of a mountain. The White Bear instructed the girl to go into the very centre of the cave, kneel, and place her palm flat on the floor. The girl did so, and found her hand on a thick iron ring. She pulled the ring, and up came a trap door large enough for the White Bear to climb through.

The girl and her companion walked through a cold stone corridor until they reached a large and rather grand looking door. On this door the White Bear pounded three times with his forepaws. Immediately it was opened by a young man dressed in the smart uniform of a valet.

'Sir! You have returned!'

'Indeed.'

'And with a companion?'

The valet seemed a little alarmed to see the pretty young girl with his master.

'And what of - ?'

'My guest will need a room, of course,' interrupted the White Bear. 'Please light the fires in the Green Suite and make sure it is prepared for her. She will be staying with us for some time.'

The girl was shown through the underground palace to a set of rooms complete with more comforts than she could ever have wished for. The bed was surrounded with rich velvet curtains; she had her own bathroom with shelves full of scented salts and dried petals; her drawing room's chairs and settees were softer by far than her bed back at home.

'I shan't mind staying here,' she thought to herself. 'I am sure that the White Bear does not mean to keep his word. He will never release me, not even in a year and a day. But I should like to stay here for ever.'

She was glad her father had not known the true nature of her deal with the White Bear. He would only worry when she didn't come home after a year and a day.

When evening fell, the girl went to meet the White Bear in the dining hall for supper.

'Please help me understand, sir,' she heard the valet plead. 'What am I to tell the Princess if she visits?'

'You must trust me,' the White Bear insisted. 'Keep the Princess away from me, and do not mention the girl. Trust me.'

The girl opened the door fully. The valet was sitting at the dining table with his master, head in hands. At the sound of the door, he leapt to his feet, hurried over to the sideboard and busied himself with the wine.

Later, when the girl was tucked up in bed, she heard footsteps somewhere close to her room. She thought she heard whispers too, but her mind was heavy and she could not be sure. As she drifted off to sleep, she thought she felt a slight breeze as though the covers had been lifted for a moment.

The next morning, the girl woke up alone beneath her feather-filled quilt, but the pillow next to hers had been disturbed.

'Tonight I must stay awake,' the girl told herself. 'I must know if the White Bear slips into my bed at night.'

So that night, after the fire had died and she had blown out all her candles, she sat up in the dark, eyes wide and sightless, refusing to settle.

Again she heard footsteps, and definitely whispers, and then the door to her outer room opening, then the door to her bedroom.

The girl slid silently down beneath the covers and waited. Someone did indeed slip into bed by her side, but it was not the bulky form of a large bear. It was a tall figure, a slender figure, the figure of a man. The girl shut her eyes tight. She supposed it was the valet, but she could not work out how that fit in with the White Bear's plan. If the White Bear intended to marry her, why would he send his valet into her bed? Was he testing her?

Eventually the girl drifted off to sleep, and when she woke the man had gone. She pondered the strange situation all day. She went down to the valet's room and saw him polishing his boots. He stood when he saw her, looking a little alarmed.

'Good morning, Miss. Can I help you?'

He didn't look quite so tall as his shadow had at night.

'Oh, no. I am not used to this place yet. I must have lost my bearings.'

'Shall I escort you to the drawing room, Miss?'

She followed the valet away from the servants' quarters, wondering if there was another man in the house.

Once again she stayed awake in the night. The footsteps and whispers came, then the doors, then the figure in her bed.

'You are awake, my Lady,' said a familiar voice.

'Yes, my Lord.'

'Then I can only apologise. I am forbidden by magic to disclose the details of my plight, but please be patient with me. A year and a day is all I ask. A year and a day, and then you will be free to return to your family and their newfound wealth. I beg you to stay with me.'

The girl thought about this. The White Bear needed her help. Then, she supposed, they would fall in love, and when a year and a day was through they would have no desire to be parted, and she would stay with this man who was sometimes a bear for ever.

'I cannot refuse you, my Lord. You, who have given such wealth to my family. I have only one request. I have seen your face of the day, the mask of the White Bear that you wear so well. Might I see your face of the night?'

'Alas, my Lady, I cannot allow that.'

So the girl and the White Bear each fell into their solitary sleep in the dark.

Once again, when the rising sun lit up the room and woke the girl, she was alone.

On this morning, the White Bear approached the girl with an offer.

'As long as we are together by nightfall, there is no need for me to keep you from your family.'

'I have told you before, my Lord, that I am willing to sacrifice my old life. You have given my family the wealth you promised, and I intend to give you the year and a day that I promised.'

'I am sure you will honour our agreement,' said the White Bear with a gracious bow, 'but I cannot let you be parted so solidly from those you love.'

It was decided that they would visit the girl's family that very day. The girl climbed onto the back of the White Bear, and off they went.

The girl's family now lived in a house large enough that each child had their own room. They lived comfortably, and as soon as the girl arrived home they threw a most impressive feast to celebrate.

'But I must be gone again before the sun sets,' said the girl.

Now, the girl's mother was curious about this, and she took her daughter aside and began to question her about her time with the White Bear. Soon enough, the girl had told her mother all about his nightly visits.

'Then you cannot stay!' gasped her mother. 'He is surely a troll, luring you into his cave and trapping you there with false promises!'

The girl waved such silly fears aside, but her mother pressed a candle into her hands and insisted,

'Take this. Hide it with you, and when he next comes to you at night, wait for him to fall asleep and get a good look at him. You have the right to know who is lying in your bed.'

That night, when the girl and the White Bear had returned to the underground palace, she listened out again for the footsteps. The whispers this time were barely whispers. She could hear the voice of the valet.

'I urge you not to continue with this foolishness. I cannot imagine what has possessed you to – '

'I have told you time after time to trust me and to say nothing.'

'With respect, *Sir*, I am not here to keep your sordid secrets.'

'You are here to do exactly as you are told. Now leave me be.'

The girl closed her eyes tight, the candle hidden in her nightgown, and tried to imitate the breath of sleep.

She waited for a full hour, to be sure the White Bear was truly asleep. Then she lit the candle and held it over him.

The boy she saw was beautiful. His hair was white like his fur, and the bones of his face held something of the bear's nobility. Unable to resist, the girl leant over and kissed his mouth.

A drop of tallow fell from her melting candle onto his nightshirt. The boy woke up.

With a cry of horror he pushed the girl away from him.

'What are you doing?' he demanded. His hand flew to his mouth and he said, softly this time, 'What have you done?'

'I'm sorry, my love,' sobbed the girl. 'I could not resist. We are meant to be, I know it! At the end of all this we will be together! But I had to see you, my darling. I had to see your true face. Please forgive me!'

The boy looked at the girl, at her candle and her tears.

'I am engaged,' he told her, 'but my fiancé's mother has cursed me to live in the body of a bear by day. I can only break the spell if I sleep next to the same soul every night for a year and a day, but they must never see me and I must never touch them, and I am forbidden from explaining my situation until it is over. Now,' he touched his lips once more. 'Now you cannot break the spell for me.' He drew a deep, trembling breath. 'I apologise a thousand times for the part I have tried to make you play in this. I wish things could have been different. I should not have allowed myself to use you in this way. It was selfish and cruel, and I am terribly sorry.'

Head bowed, weeping quietly, the boy left the room.

When morning came, the valet knocked on the girl's door.

'Where is he?' she asked.

'He has decided to return to his fiancé and her mother, in the castle East of the Sun and West of the Moon. He intends to beg for another way to lift the curse. I am to escort you back to your family, and offer you his deepest apologies for involving you in his affairs.'

The girl was distraught. She could not return to her family, not without her love. Rejecting the valet's offer, the girl set out alone to find the castle. She walked until the sun was at its highest point in the sky, when she came across an old lady sitting on the steps of a little hut.

'Can you help me, Wise One? I am searching for the castle that is East of the Sun and West of the Moon.'

'And what business have you there, child?'

41

'I must save my love, the White Bear, who is being forced to marry the daughter of the very troll who cursed him!'

'You are the White Bear's love?'

'Indeed I am.'

'The stories paint you quite differently, child. But gossip is gossip, and I have no time for it. Take my horse, for it knows the way, and ride to my sister in the East. She may be able to help you.'

The girl thanked the old woman and rode to the East. She rode until the sun began to set, and then came across a second hut with another old woman sitting at the steps.

'Greetings, child!' the woman called. 'I see my sister has sent you. What can I do for you?'

The girl jumped down from the horse and knelt by the woman.

'Please, Wise One, you must help me find the castle that lies East of the Sun and West of the Moon. My love, the White Bear, has been cursed by a troll and will be forced to marry her daughter if I do not reach him in time!'

The woman looked the girl up and down.

'The White Bear's love? I think you have been done an injustice, my dear. But gossip is only gossip, after all. Take my mule, for it knows the way, and ride to the West Wind. He will help you, I am sure of it.'

Off the girl rode once more, rode until the moon was high in the sky, until she came to where the West Wind rested.

'Greetings, my dear!' the West Wind called from the branches of a tree. 'I see the sisters have sent you to me. How can I be of service?'

'Sir, I am the one true love of the White Bear! He was to marry me after a year and a day, but now he has been taken to the castle East of the Sun and West of the Moon. There he will be forced to marry the daughter of the troll who cursed him. You must take me there so I can save him from this terrible fate!'

The West Wind frowned down at the girl.

'You are betrothed to the White Bear? My dear, gossip can be so unkind. But it is only gossip, and we shall speak no more of it. I have rested here long enough, I think. Let us be off.'

The girl climbed onto the back of the West Wind, and he blew them far and wide for the rest of the night and the whole of the day. As the sun began to set again, the West Wind landed in the grounds of a grand castle. He settled himself in a tall fir tree.

'My dear, I am exhausted,' he said to the girl. 'I hope I have landed in time. Go to your White Bear, and may you share endless years of love together.'

The girl ran to the castle doors, where stood a short, squat young woman. Her nose was a great hook with a bulbous mole on one nostril, and her mouth stretched too wide and too thin across her broad face.

'Are you the one the White Bear must marry?' said the girl boldly to this troll of a woman.

'The White Bear?' The troll's mouth gaped into a horrid leer. 'Are you here to save him?'

'Indeed I am.' The girl drew herself up to her full height and cast her eyes up and down the stout body. 'Would you stop me?'

The troll looked down, an extra chin squeezing its way out between her head and neck.

'Though the situation pains me, I must allow you in.'

The girl, who had expected the beast to put up a bigger fight, pushed past and made her way into the castle, up the twisting stone stairs, and into the tower that was the White Bear's room. The sun having now set, she was faced with the figure of the pale young man that she had found so irresistible. She gazed at him, breathless, and prepared herself for his embrace.

'What are you doing here?' the White Bear asked.

'My love, I have travelled from your home to this terrible place in order to release you from your foul contract with this troll.' She waved a hand at the bloated figure of the fiancé who had followed her upstairs. 'The West Wind will take us both home, darling one, and together we will find a way to break this curse. You do not have to bind yourself to a monster!'

The White Bear turned from the girl to the troll and back again.

'Monster?' he asked.

'Yes. This troll whose mother has cursed you.'

The White Bear crossed the room, arms outstretched, and embraced his one true love.

The girl could not speak.

The White Bear made no attempt to hide the fury on his face.

'What right have you to barge into my sleeping quarters, insult my Princess, and demand my love?'

The girl stepped back, horrified at the vision of her beautiful boy in the arms of the hideous woman.

'Less than a fortnight has passed since I first laid eyes on you. How do you expect that to compete with the years of love I have shared with this fine young lady? I am truly sorry for taking you away as I did, but I have made my apologies and I will not allow you to speak of my future wife as you have done.'

And so the West Wind blew, the mule trotted, the horse galloped, and the girl returned home with an empty heart and bruised pride.

The White Bear's valet arrived at the castle East of the Sun and West of the Moon the morning after the girl's arrival and abrupt departure.

'Forgive me, Sir, for having listened at your door, but I heard your conversation with our young lady guest before your departure. If I understand the terms of the enchantment correctly, I may have a solution for this horrid dilemma.'

The White Bear's soft ears twitched.

'You crept along the halls at night in darkness, Sir. I was aware of your changed form, but I never saw you. And you have not told me of the curse, for I overheard it on my own. Since I am already required to reside with you in order to perform my duties as your valet, I see no reason why you should not be married to your true love in a year and a day.'

The White Bear's muzzle shifted in the manner of a human smile.

## THOU TALK'ST OF NOTHING

Amalda's mother married a man who took great delight in demanding the impossible and complaining when it could not be done. One day, when Amalda was packing her school bag, he whipped the books from her hands and slapped into them instead a sieve.

'What's this nonsense?' she demanded. 'I don't want to be late again.'

'Take this to the Well at the World's End and fill it with water for me. And if you don't bring it back full, you're in for a hiding, my girl.'

'I'm not your girl,' Amalda snapped. 'And what's wrong with the tap? *And* I have school.'

But the stepfather kept hold of the books and took her bag and shoes as well, so that even if Amalda did run off to school she would only be told off for not having her homework or any of her workbooks, and for wearing her trainers. The stepfather was much larger than Amalda, who was less than one third of his age and smaller than her peers to boot. So she sighed heavily, took the sieve, and asked him where this Well was.

'Where? Idiot girl,' he bellowed. 'Find it yourself.'

And he shoved her out of the house and slammed the door.

'Stupid man,' muttered Amalda to herself as she stomped up the road.

The corner shop was owned by an old man called Rakesh who liked to tell Amalda stories about his childhood, stories so fanciful that she never believed a single one. But perhaps he might know something about the Well at the World's End. It was as good a place to start as any. And even if he didn't, she had a few coins in her pocket and would be able to buy some sweets.

'Hello, Mr Rakesh,' she said.

'Running late, are you?'

'I'm not going to school today.'

'No? Education is important, young lady. When I was your age I was delighted to go to school! Say, did I ever tell you - ?'

'I'm sorry to be rude, but I can't listen to a story today.'

Rakesh looked a little upset, but he knew the girl meant no harm.

'Unless you can tell me about the Well at the World's End?' she asked. 'My stupid stepdad wants me to fill this sieve there.'

'Fill a sieve?' The old man chuckled. 'That's quite some task.'

'I told you he was stupid,' said Amalda. 'Can you help me, then?'

Rakesh leaned over the counter and beckoned the girl closer.

'The Well at the World's End is a very special place,' he told her. 'I have been there only once, though I know the way. First you must go through a happy memory, then you turn off at minor illness and keep going until you see future possibilities, and it's there on the right. You can't miss it.'

Amalda rolled her eyes.

'That's the silliest load of rubbish you've ever told me, Mr Rakesh,' she said firmly.

The old man shrugged, his dark eyes twinkling.

'If you want to get to the Well, that's the only way I know. If not,' he pointed north-east. 'I believe your school is that-a-way.'

Amalda bought a tube of wine gums and thanked Rakesh. Out on the pavement, she sucked the first of her sweets.

The sugary flavour spread across her tongue and skipped around her mouth. When she was a lot littler, she had been on holiday with her mum and her real dad, somewhere by the seaside. She couldn't think where. Her dad promised her an ice-cream, and they walked hand in hand along the promenade by the beach to an ice-cream hut. It was closed, and Amalda was bitterly disappointed. They couldn't see another hut or an ice-cream van anywhere, only souvenir shops selling plastic buckets and blow up dolphins. Her dad let her jump up onto his back, and he jogged with her – still in his beach trunks – away from the beach and towards the town until they found a newsagent's.

'Here we are!' he said. 'I bet they'll have a lolly for you in here!'

But their freezer was on the blink.

Amalda remembered being close to tears by this point. Silly baby, she thought to herself now. Crying over ice-cream.

Desperate to please his little girl, Amalda's dad had bought a curly plastic straw and a tube of wine gums, and he skewered the sweets on the end of the straw like some sugary kebab and presented it to her with a flourish.

'A unique, chewy lolly for my favourite little girl,' he said to her.

It was nothing like an ice-cream or a cold fruit ice-lolly, of course, but she liked the straw and her dad was so silly about the whole thing that it made her giggle. Hand in hand with her dad, and licking her sweets-on-a-straw as if it really was a lolly, Amalda had gone back to the beach happy.

Now, Amalda sneezed. She fumbled in the pocket of her school blazer for a tissue. Her head felt a bit fuzzy, so she sat down. It was then that she realised she was no longer on the pavement outside Rakesh's corner shop. She wasn't quite sure where she was, but she was sitting on a soft orange cushion nearly as big as her bed at home. A nap sounded like quite a nice idea, but she'd only got up an hour ago. Her eyelids were heavy and the odd hot tear leaked down her face. She wasn't crying, but trying not to sneeze made her eyes water.

She looked up at her surroundings to distract herself from feeling groggy and saw a man coming over to her who looked younger than her mum and stepfather. He was wearing pale blue scrubs and clean white shoes.

'How are you feeling, pet?' he asked her.

'Okay,' she said. She sounded stuffy and her nostrils felt sore and tender when she blew her nose.

'You just need plenty of rest. Can I get you something warm to drink? Hot milk or chocolate? Or do you like tea?'

She wanted to ask for tea, because it was a much more grown up drink and she wanted him to know that she was just short, not a really little kid. But hot chocolate sounded much more comforting.

'Are you a doctor?' she asked when she had a cosy mug between her hands.

'I'm a nurse,' he said.

'I used to want to be a nurse,' Amalda told the man.

'Do you not anymore?'

She shook her head.

'I thought nurse meant a girl doctor,' she said. 'I want to be a doctor.' Then, in case she had offended him, she added, 'But anything in medicine would be okay. I could be a nurse or a dentist or an optician.'

'You could indeed,' said the young nurse, smiling fondly at her. 'The world is your oyster. And maybe I'll see you working here one day, Dr Amalda.'

Amalda puffed up at the thought of being a real grown up doctor.

'Yeah,' she said. 'Maybe.'

Then quite suddenly she caught sight of an old stone Well with a wooden bucket hanging from it.

'Oh! Is that the Well at the World's End?'

The nurse followed her pointing finger to their right and saw it too.

'Looks like it,' he said. 'Bye then, Dr Amalda.'

'Bye, Mr Friendly Nurse,' she said, because she didn't know his name.

She jumped up and ran over to the Well with her sieve, and the cushion and mug and nurse dissolved behind her.

The stones of the Well's wall were covered in moss, and Amalda's hands slipped and slid when she leant over to peer down. She couldn't see the bottom, but she supposed there must be water down there somewhere. Just to make sure, she picked up a little stone, dropped it in the Well and turned her ear downwards to hear the plop. It took several seconds, but there it was, a plop that echoed back up the walls to her. The plop was shortly followed by a ribbet, then a croaky voice singing.

'Come down the Well, my hinny, my heart.

Come down the Well, my young darling.

Follow the stone to the water deep

At the bottom of the Well at the World's End.'

Amalda leant further over and squinted into the darkness.

'Hello?' she called. 'Who's down there?'

'Just a little someone who has been dying to meet you, dear,' replied the croaky voice.

Amalda shivered. It didn't sound like a friendly voice, and she didn't want to talk to it. She said no more, and set about lowering the bucket to the water. She heard it hit the wet surface and felt the weight of it pulling as its lip dipped below and it began to fill. When it felt like no more water was pouring in, she pulled the bucket back up. It wobbled as she pulled, slopping water back down the Well, but there was still plenty enough to fill the sieve. She unhooked the bucket and put it down on the ground by her feet, then considered the sieve.

'What shall I do with you?' she asked it. 'I'll have to line you with something, I suppose.'

Then out of the bucket hopped a small green frog. It was a very pretty colour, and its moist skin gleamed handsomely in the sunlight.

'Hello there,' she said to it. 'Sorry. I didn't mean to disturb you. Shall I put you back into the Well? I just need to get some of this water in my sieve, then I'll send you back down in the bucket, okay?'

She quite wanted to hold the little thing, but she thought she'd heard somewhere that the oils on her skin could damage the frog's, so she didn't.

'Not for me, that dank old Well, no, no, not for me,' said the frog, and it was the same voice that had sung to her. Suddenly the animal didn't look so sweet.

'Okay then,' she said, and went back to considering the sieve, hoping it would hop off and leave her be.

The moss on the stone could help, she thought. She began to pull tufts of it out of the cracks and stuff them into the bottom of the sieve. Then she poured in a little water. It was mightily better than the sieve without moss, but still water leaked out. She would never manage to carry enough home to her stepfather like this.

While she worked, the frog hopped closer and leered at her.

'I can help you, little lovely,' it croaked. 'If you will promise to take me home with you, I can help you fix that sieve into a nice bucket.'

'No, thank you,' said Amalda.

It was only a small creature, but the frog made her nervous. She was scared to anger it by being rude, but she didn't want it to talk to her any more.

Trying to ignore the frog, she focused her mind back on the problem of the sieve. The ground around her was the rusty red of clay. Perhaps that would stick well to the moss and line the sieve. She crouched down and scooped up handfuls of the clay to smear along the bottom of the vessel.

'Clever girl, clever girl,' croaked the frog. It lashed its tongue out close to Amalda's hand, and she couldn't help but shudder. The frog laughed a deep, ugly laugh. 'I'm just playing, sweetheart, just playing. Don't be scared.' Its tongue slobbered again, even closer this time.

Amalda jumped to her feet, smoothed the last handful of clay across the bottom of her makeshift bowl and tried it with water again, desperately hoping that it would work and she could leave this loathsome creature's presence.

Not a single leak.

Amalda breathed a sigh of relief and, carrying the sieve carefully in both hands, began to walk away from the Well.

'What about me, my hinny, my heart?
What about me, my young darling?
Is this how you leave me, alone and unloved,
Trapped by the Well at the World's End?'

Amalda ran.

Rakesh had not told her how to get home from the Well, but as she ran Amalda found herself in a familiar park, not too far from her house. Though there was no sign of the Well or the frog anymore, she didn't stop running until she was at her door.

She knocked hard, her heart pumping frantically under her ribs.

'Where have you been?' the stepfather demanded when he opened the door. 'It's nearly dark. Your mother was getting worried.'

'If she's so worried about me, why did she let me go?' Amalda shouted back.

She thrust the sieve into the man's hands and ran upstairs to her room. There, she curled up on her bed, hid her head under her pillow, and tried to think of Dad and wine gums and kind nurses and her adult self as a doctor. Giant, threatening frogs loomed at the edge of her imagination, but she swung an equally giant scalpel at them and scared them off.

She must have drifted from waking dreams to sleeping dreams, for when she opened her eyes it was pitch black and something was squelching and shuffling outside her door. She held her breath and hoped she would stop hearing things, but she had no such luck. A soft croaking began.

'Open your door, my hinny, my heart.
Open your door, my young darling.
Remember the words that you and I spoke
Down by the Well at the World's End.'

Amalda could not help herself. She wanted to be brave and deal with him alone, but instead she screamed.

In an instant her mother and stepfather were at the door, the light in her room was blazing, and the frog was inside, sitting in a little damp circle on her carpet.

'How did that get in?' asked her mother.

'All this racket over a stupid reptile,' snarled the stepfather. 'Just chuck it out the window.'

'Wait,' said the frog. 'Your daughter made a promise to me. I helped her fill her sieve, and in return she was to take me home.'

Despite her fear, Amalda found her voice.

'I never agreed to that! I filled the sieve on my own!'

She glared at her parents, and the frog too looked at them with his big, bulging eyes. How had she ever thought he was a dear little creature? He was a squat, bulbous thing, invading her home and her life.

Her mother held her gaze for a moment, and Amalda felt hopeful. But then the eyes of comfort turned instead to the stepfather, leaving the decision to him.

He snorted.

'The girl couldn't have thought of using clay herself. When has she been good for anything? She's lying.'

'I'm not!' Amalda protested.

'Girls must keep their promises.'

Amalda pleaded silently with her mother, but her mother looked at her feet and did nothing.

The frog licked its lips.

> 'Take me to bed, my hinny, my heart.
> Take me to bed, my young darling.
> Your parents command it and I must be paid
> For my help at the Well at the World's End.'

The stepfather waited, his arms crossed firmly over his chest. Her mother stood with her head down. The frog hopped closer.

Amalda shuddered, then bent down and let the frog squirm onto her palm. Satisfied, her parents switched off the bedroom light and left.

Amalda tipped the frog onto her pillow, trying to swallow the sickness in her throat. She didn't want this thing anywhere near her, let alone in her room. Her window was in the wall furthest from her bed, so she went and stood there and looked out at the stars, all the while listening for shuffles and squelches in case the frog hopped off her bed and tried to approach her.

Her feet began to ache.

Her legs grew stiff.

Her eyes tried to close.

Amalda pushed through the desire to sleep and kept her vigil by the window until, many long hours later, the sun finally rose and flooded the room with a golden glow. The frog on her pillow stirred. Its mouth smacked wetly.

'Still so shy, dear one?' it asked, and it cleared its throat with a croak and began to sing again.

'Come closer to me, my hinny, my heart.

Come closer to me, my – '

'That does it!' cried Amalda.

She did not want to hear what this grotesque invader was going to ask of her next. She had a little desk in her room, and on her little desk were pens and pencils and paper and a big pair of scissors. She snatched up the blades, marched over to her bed, and sliced off the frog's head.

There on her bed sat a man of a similar age to the friendly nurse. There was something of the frog in his wide mouth and bulging eyes. He licked his lips.

'Mother!' he called. 'Father! Come to your daughter's room!'

Once more the two burst in, wondering what was the cause of this new commotion. They stared at the young man, and at Amalda, and could say nothing.

'Your daughter has broken my curse,' said the man. 'I was turned into a frog by a cruel witch, and the only way to become myself again was to have a beautiful girl obey me for one night, until the sun rose, and then to chop off my head in the morning.'

Amalda's parents were stunned. She, however, simply folded her arms and sniffed.

'I think I need to say sorry to Mr Rakesh. This is much stupider than anything he's ever come out with.'

The frog man licked his lips again.

'Now that you have freed me, love, I shall marry you. You shall be my Princess.'

'I shall not!' Amalda stamped her foot and turned to her mother. 'Mum, get this creepy man out of my room.'

The stepfather held up his hand.

'Princess?' he asked.

The frog man nodded.

'I am a Prince,' he said. 'You will be well provided for, of course, when your daughter marries me.'

Amalda could all but see the gold coins shining in the stepfather's eyes. She looked at her mother, who refused to meet her eye.

'I can't marry you!' she cried. 'I'm twelve. And I hate you anyway. Mum? Mum, what are you doing? Get rid of him!'

The frog man's smile widened and he reached for Amalda's arm.

'Don't touch me!' she screamed, and lashed out with the scissors she still held, cutting a deep gash into his forearm. She held the blades before her, her only defence against the three adults, and ran from her room.

She ran out of the house, up the road, and into the little corner shop, where the old man Rakesh sat behind his counter reading his morning newspaper.

'What on earth is the matter with you, Amalda?' he asked as she threw herself through the door.

She burst into furious tears, and the man took her in his arms like he had done his own daughters, sons and grandchildren, and he rocked her gently and muttered soothing things into her ear until she calmed down. When she could speak again, she told him everything, right from eating the wine gum on the pavement outside, up to cutting the horrible frog man's arm with her scissors.

'Well now,' said Rakesh, 'I think you've been very brave. I don't know if many children your age could have fought off a grown man with a pair of scissors.'

He smiled encouragingly, and she felt her face smiling back.

'That's it,' he said. 'As long as you can smile, you have won.'

The bell above the shop door jingled.

'Whatever it is can wait, Aziz,' said Rakesh to the young man who had walked in. 'I have a young hero recovering here.'

Aziz looked at the little girl in his grandfather's arms.

'Dr Amalda,' he said.

'Mr Friendly Nurse,' Amalda said with a sniff.

It did not take long for Amalda to settle in with her new family, who looked after her just as well as her real dad had, which needless to say was much better than her mother and stepfather.

As for the frog man, the witch Rakesh turned him into a slug, along with his two would-be accomplices. And this time, he gave the curse no clause with which it could be broken. The three slugs were thrown into the Well at the World's End, and whether they live there still, clinging to the stone, or whether they drowned in the water at the bottom, there is no one who knows or cares.

## SHE DRIVETH O'ER A SOLDIER'S NECK

There was once a young soldier coming home from war, a pack on his back, a sword at his side, and well-worn boots on his feet. Seeing a lone tree near the road, he thought he might rest a while for he had nowhere much to be and nothing much waiting for him anywhere. When he got to the tree, he saw there a woman sitting alone and making a plain wool rug with a hook.

'Am I so near a town?' the soldier wondered aloud. 'I must be, if here sits a woman, whiling away the hours, who must live somewhere.'

'The town is not so near, I'm afraid,' said the woman. 'I am Betha, and I have long since been banished, so that now I do not live anywhere at all.'

'For what sin would a woman so young and beautiful be sent alone into the world?' asked the soldier, for he took a shine to Betha's silver hair and her sweet voice.

'Don't mind about that, good soldier,' said Betha. 'But I wonder, perhaps you could help me? You look like a man who deserves the world, and yet here you are with boots that would fall apart as soon as stepped on. I would see you wealthy, dear soldier.'

Well now, the soldier puffed out his chest to think that Betha saw an image of a hero before her, and he lifted his head with pride and said to her,

'A soldier does not fight for money, dear Betha. A soldier fights for his country, for justice, for the good of those such as yourself who cannot fight for themselves.'

Betha fluttered her eyelashes and tossed her long silver hair behind her shoulders.

'You truly are an honourable man. Then perhaps you will help me without the reward.'

'For you I will do anything, sweet Betha.'

It happened that the tree Betha sat beneath was dead and hollow, and with a gaping hole in the top.

'I have lost my tinderbox inside this tree,' Betha told the soldier. 'It is silly, I know, but someone dear to me gave me the thing, and I should like to have it back. But you see, this tree is guarded by strong magics, and nobody can enter more than once. If I go down to fetch my tinderbox, I will die. Would you be kind enough to fetch it for me?'

The soldier was more than happy to do so, for he hoped to keep Betha's favour. She was such a pretty thing, after all. From his pack he took a length of rope, and tying it about his waist he instructed Betha to hold on to the end that he might lower himself down into the tree to look for her tinderbox.

'But it isn't quite so simple as that,' said Betha. 'Now, at the bottom of the tree you will find a room with a chest, and a guard atop it. That chest is full of copper, I believe, but that will not interest you. If you get the guard to stand on this rug, they will not bother you. Of course, they guard only the chest, so that does not matter.

'Beyond the chest is another door, and through there is another room with another chest, filled with silver, I think, not that you care for such things. Again, the guard will only harm you if you try to get into the chest, but you will pass through easily.

'Beyond the second chest is another door, and through there another room, another guard, guarding gold, if memory serves me correctly. Now, it is in this room that I lost my tinderbox. It may be atop the chest, so you may need to coax the guard onto the rug before you can pick it up. But, silly me, the guard will only fight if you try to open the chest. You will not need my rug at all.

'Now. Are you quite ready?'

The soldier's mind was swimming with copper coin, silver cups, golden crowns, and it was all he could do not to gape openly at the thought of such riches.

'Perhaps I should take your rug, just in case. If your tinderbox is on the chest, and I touch the lid, perhaps the guard will think I am trying to open the chest.'

Betha nodded.

'You are right to be cautious,' she said. 'Far better to be safe than sorry, wise soldier.'

And so she gave the soldier the rug, and lowered him down into the first room.

The soldier could not see at first, for all his squinting in the dark. He could make out a shadowed shape, which he headed towards, thinking it to be the chest and the guard.

'Are you going to stab me again, Mister?'

The guard peered into the darkness, but he could not see.

'Who is that?' he called at the shadow.

A small flame lit up the chest, and sitting on it holding a tallow candle was a girl no more than eight years old.

'My sister isn't here this time. Do you remember my sister? She was only three. You didn't stab her. She was crying over me, and you shook her to shut her up. Do you remember? But she wouldn't stop, so you put your own hands to her throat.'

The room became a village on fire, and the soldier saw himself, back when his boots were new and polished, driving his sword through the little girl's abdomen and squeezing the life from her sister's neck.

'I haven't the time for these memories!' he cried, and the image faded.

He picked up the little girl and put her on Betha's rug. Then he opened up the chest, and sure enough, there was a pile of shining copper coins. He started to stuff as many as he could into his pockets, but, remembering the silver in the next room, he filled only his left pocket.

Then the soldier pulled the rug from under the little girl's feet and went into the second room.

The darkness was not so thick here, but a fog filled the space so that the soldier could only guess at where to put his feet. He shuffled forwards, coins clinking against his leg, until the hazy image of a block and a figure appeared less than an arm's length from him. He laid the rug on the floor at his feet.

'Whoever you are, step down onto this rug,' he demanded. 'I must get into that chest.'

It was with many voices, all around him, that he was answered.

'We all want things in this world,' they said. 'We wanted you to guide us to safety with your torch, but you left us all.'

The soldier felt the bite of an ocean-born wind, could smell the salt in the air. The torch in his hand smouldered, and he listened to the screams of adults and children alike as they lost their footing on the treacherous cliff path, lost without the light he had extinguished.

'Stop these visions!' he cried. 'Why are you tormenting me with this witchcraft?'

The sounds of the sea diminished, and the fog in the room cleared. He knew the woman who sat on the chest, hair a tangle, dress torn and marked with blood. The promise of safety, of a guiding light, had been made to her for all of her people.

'The real question,' said she, 'is why should you escape this torment? After all, we did not escape. You led us to our deaths.'

With a hard shove, he pushed the woman from the chest to the rug and flung wide the lid.

Just as Betha had said, it was silver in this chest. He threw away the copper, not noticing when the hard coins struck the woman on the floor, and filled both pockets with silver trinkets. But remembering the room of gold beyond, he saved room in his pack for more.

The woman was slight, and it was easy to pull the rug from beneath her and send her rolling over the cold stone ground. The soldier rolled up the rug and moved on through the next door.

This time he was blinded by the brightness of the underground cavern. He could not see what it was that gave off such light, but he shielded his eyes and staggered through the room anyway, until he stubbed a toe on something solid.

'It has been some time, has it not?'

The light died, but the soldier, recognising the voice, kept his face covered.

'Why do you cover your eyes? Can you not stomach the sight of me?'

'What will I see if I look?' the soldier asked, and his voice trembled. 'Will I see you as you always were?'

'You will see me as you left me.'

The soldier reached out a hand and felt for the chest, felt for its lid. His fingers found the cold flesh of another, and he fell to the floor with a cry.

'Open your eyes.'

His quivering hands fell, and his eyelids lifted.

The man on the chest was young and strong, and his soft mouth gently smiled. He wore a military uniform, identical to the soldier's own, and shining black boots. He would have been the very picture of protection, had it not been for the gash across his neck.

'Do you remember what you swore? What you swore on our mother's grave?'

The soldier licked sweat from his lip and tried to speak, but his voice failed.

'You swore that you would always look after me. Did you know how I always admired you?'

The soldier nodded his head, and felt the hot tears spilling down his clammy cheeks.

'Do you remember my eyes, the last time you looked at me? Do you remember what you saw?'

The soldier's throat was tight. His breath was short and ragged.

'I saw...' he choked. 'I saw...'

'You saw my pain. My disbelief. My horror that you could do such a thing to your own kin.'

'No more of this!' the soldier cried, and he swung his sword at the image of his young brother. The young man tumbled down, and when he tried to rise the soldier threw the rug over his head and held him, writhing beneath the fabric, until he moved no more.

He wiped his face on his sleeve and opened the chest.

There lay more gold than he had ever hoped to set eyes on, and he tossed away the silver from his pockets and filled every pouch he had with gold goblets, stuffed his sleeves and boots full of coins and chains, piled ring after ring onto every finger.

When he could carry no more, he bent to retrieve the rug, thinking he might need it to pass back through the other rooms. The image of his brother had vanished, and instead a small tarnished tinderbox lay on the rug. Until he saw it, the soldier had forgotten all about Betha's request. He picked it up, the ugly old thing. It was dull and small and nothing compared to the riches that weighed him down. Such a curious thing to desire, of all the things down here.

With the rug under one arm and the box in his hand, the soldier made his way back to the first room without any more haunting visions.

'Betha, my darling,' he called up through the hole above him. 'Pull me up! I have your little trinket here.'

And so Betha pulled on the rope and the soldier returned to the world above.

She saw his bulging pockets, heard the clinking of his pack, and looked to see if he had the decency to show any shame. He was staring down at the tinderbox in his palm and, not knowing how she studied his face, he asked her,

'Why do you want this thing?'

'I told you,' said she, holding out her hand for the box. 'It was given to me by someone special.'

The soldier laughed and tossed the box up and down without a care.

'He can't be so special. What kind of a gift is this for such a beautiful young lady?'

Betha frowned and tried to snatch the box from him, but he held it firm in his fist out of her reach.

'It is no business of yours what I want with the box,' she snapped. 'You have your treasure, honourable soldier. Now give me my box and be on your way.'

The soldier did not like Betha's tone. He was only teasing her, after all, and he had been so kind to take the time to fetch her stupid knick-knack from the underground cavern. And hadn't she thought him brave, and handsome, no doubt, the way she had blinked her eyes and smiled at him?

'No need to get so feisty, sweet Betha.' He reached out to touch her soft cheek. 'Shall we kiss and make up? Then you can have the silly thing.'

Betha slapped his hand away and made another grab for the tinderbox. The soldier laughed and held it high above his head.

'Just one kiss, darling, and you shall have the box and I shall be on my way.'

'I would die before I would let you have my lips, soldier.'

'Very well.'

And so the soldier drew his sword and sliced off Betha's pretty head.

*

The nearest town was splendid indeed, and when the soldier arrived he had such a great many treasures with him that he was taken for a young lord and given the best rooms, right next to the palace where the King lived with his Queen and daughter.

The soldier had a fine time spending his money. He bought fine clothes that befitted his new image, and he showered fine gifts on all the fine lords and ladies that he took to be his friends. Every night he dined heavily and drank his way through the most costly bottles of wine, then danced until dawn at the nightly balls thrown by the King.

It was in these times that he socialised with those close to the King, and he learned of the Princess.

'She is the most beautiful thing you would ever set eyes on,' they told him. 'But set eyes on her you never shall, for it was prophesised that she would marry a commoner, so he keeps her locked away from us all lest she should meet one of our servants and fall in love.'

This cheered the soldier greatly, for despite his wealth, and despite what his new friends thought of him, he was not of noble birth. What other commoner would have the chance to meet the Princess, besides the one who was thought to be noble?

It was then that the soldier began to try and find favour with the King, hoping to meet his daughter. After all, she must be married eventually.

Before the soldier begged an audience with the King, he first took all his copper coins to a sculptor.

'I wish you to melt these coins for me, good fellow, and with them sculpt a shining statue of the Queen that is as beautiful as her hair' – for the Queen was famed for her long copper curls – 'and I will pay you in silver.'

Now, the sculptor had never seen so many coins before, and thinking that surely only a lord of great importance could own such a sum, he set to work immediately.

When the sculpture was finished, it was indeed as fine as the Queen's shining hair. The soldier's request to see the King was granted, and he hired two men to carry in the copper Queen for him.

'Your Highness,' he addressed the King, sweeping off his hat and bowing low. 'I have come to present you with a fine gift. She is not so fine as the creature that sits at your side,' he said, adding a second low bow to the real Queen upon her throne, 'but I hope you will enjoy her.'

The King was greatly pleased with this gift, and permitted the soldier to stay for a few minutes and share some words with him and his Queen. The soldier did his best to charm them both in his limited time, and left feeling quite satisfied.

Word spread through the town of the soldier's gift to the King, and everybody agreed that if he continued to charm the King he would soon be in great favour, and perhaps would even be allowed a glimpse of the

Princess. The soldier listened to this gossip and glowed, for he was sure that he was the commoner of the prophecy.

Soon, the soldier went back to the sculptor with all that he had in silver.

'You must melt this silver down, my man, for I have another task for you. I want a sculpture of the King himself, in silver for the silver streaks of wisdom in his beard. You shall be paid in gold.'

And so the sculptor set to work, and before long the soldier was once more before the King, bowing low, with the tribute carried in behind him.

'Though fools may think gold the greatest treasure,' he said to the King, 'I know you are no fool. The silver in your beard shows your wisdom and experience, Your Highness, and that is far more valuable than gold. Please accept this gift as a token of my admiration for your firm mind.'

Though the first sculpture had been pretty, the pretty words that came with this second offering pleased the King even more. The soldier was permitted to stay longer this time, and invited to dine with the King and Queen that very evening.

He gently flattered both of them throughout the meal, and both were quite enamoured with this young lord who had so recently made such an impression on their people. When he thought they had warmed to him enough, the soldier said casually,

'I had hoped one day to bring you a third gift, but of course I cannot.'

'And why is that?' asked the King.

'It would be rather fitting, don't you think, Your Highness, to complete the set. I wanted to have made for you a golden statue of the Princess, but alas, nobody has seen her face for three years.'

Now, the King liked this young lord well enough, but he had kept his daughter hidden for good reason and was not about to let her out now, especially not to be seen by a sculptor, a commoner who might take her from him.

'I am afraid that cannot be arranged,' he told the soldier. 'You seem a loyal young man, and your gifts are appreciated. But I cannot allow anyone to see my daughter.'

The soldier finished his evening calmly, took gracious leave of his royal hosts, and returned to his rooms. There, he roared, and pounded on the wall with his fists.

You see, the soldier could never have made the golden Princess. He had thought that, being the commoner she was destined to marry, the Princess would fall in love with him as soon as they met, and he would have no need to bring the statue. The last of his gold had been used to pay the sculptor. The soldier's wealth was spent.

Unsure of what to do now, the soldier sat down on his bed to think. He reached for his pipe, and found that he had misplaced his own striker. It was then that he remembered the little tinderbox he had taken from the hollow tree. Though it was battered and torn in places, the soldier had kept his old coat for its comforting warmth, and to remind him of his days in battle. He was glad not to have discarded it, for the tarnished old tinderbox was in the pocket of this coat.

The soldier opened the box, and was surprised to find that as well as the tinder, flint and striker, the box contained a plait of auburn and silver hair, tightly entwined. He did not much care to wonder, though, and took up the tools to light his pipe.

As soon as the soldier struck a spark, a young woman appeared before him.

'Betha!' she cried with delight, then cast her eyes around the room and found only the soldier, staring, baffled by her presence.

'Sir,' she said, 'might I ask how you came by this tinderbox?'

The soldier looked at the flint and striker in his hands, and struck a second spark in case that might summon a second beautiful young woman to his room.

'Please, Sir,' she persisted. 'I am sure my appearance is startling to you, but I must know how you found the tinderbox. It belongs to someone dear to me, and I am sure they would not let it go easily. They may be in danger.'

The soldier looked at the hair in the box, then up at the lady.

'You are looking for Betha.'

Her face lit up.

'You know her? You're a friend?'

'That's right, my dear. If you wait here with me, I'm sure she will be back soon.'

He offered the lady a seat and a drink, but she was far too excited and instead took to pacing about his room and peering out of the window in the hope that she might see Betha approaching.

The soldier poured himself a glass anyway, and settled down in one of his large arm chairs.

'She will return when she returns, dear. Please do calm down. Now, might I know the name of Betha's dear friend?'

The woman stopped her agitated movement and sat down in a chair by the soldier.

'You are right, Sir. I apologise for my rudeness. Allow me to introduce myself.' She took to her feet again and curtsied. 'My name is Raina, and I am the King's daughter.'

Well now, you can imagine how the soldier's heart lifted to know that the beautiful young thing in his room was the woman destined to fall in love with him.

'My Lady,' he cried, leaping at once to his feet and answering her curtsey with a bow. 'I have heard much of your beauty and have long desired to set my eyes on you. You are even more beautiful than your mother, and I am sure your wisdom is equal to your father's.'

Raina blushed at his compliments and brushed them aside, but the soldier persisted with his flattery and insisted that she take just a small glass of wine. He talked at her for many hours, admiring her fine physical qualities and guessing at her more intangible attributes.

The night was long, and by the time the sun rose the Princess was quite anxious at Betha's absence.

'Don't worry, my dear,' said the soldier. 'Perhaps she was waylaid by some task or other. I wonder, can this box of yours send you back home?'

'Indeed,' said Raina. 'Strike the flint again, only this time make sure the tinder catches.'

'Then I shall send you home for now, dear Princess, and tomorrow night I shall summon you again.'

'And Betha will be back tomorrow?'

'Betha? Ah, yes. Betha will surely be back tomorrow.'

The soldier took his time making flowery goodbyes to Raina, and kissing the back of her hand, which she let him do once before she pulled away with a nervous laugh and asked that he light the tinder.

'Tomorrow then, darling,' said he, and sent her back home.

*

The next night, Raina waited in her chambers, having spent the day shut inside as she had been for three long years, for the tinderbox to summon her. When darkness had settled over the town, she disappeared.

This night, however, one of her maids had quite forgotten to prepare the logs for the next morning's fire. Knowing the Princess to stay awake long after she retired at night, the maid decided it would be better to briefly disturb her now, before she slept, than to wake her early next morning with her bustling. So she returned to the Princess's room with an armful of firewood and knocked upon the door. When she heard no reply, which was quite unusual for the Princess, she peeped around the door to see if perhaps her mistress had been taken ill.

In the Princess's bedroom, of course, there was no sign of the Princess.

The uproar in the palace was unbelievable. Everyone was woken and every room searched, until the King and Queen were quite hysterical and positive that their daughter had been taken forcefully from her safe place.

'Search the entire town!' cried the King. 'She must be found!'

Raina, meanwhile, had not the faintest idea of the panic she had caused by leaving the palace, and she sat once more with the soldier, waiting. When she heard the commotion of guards tramping out of the palace gates she ran straight to the window to see what was going on.

'Is it Betha?' she cried. 'She was banished from the town, you see. I do hope they haven't found her.'

She saw groups of the King's men depart down different streets, and three of them began to hammer on the front door of the soldier's building. She flew from the room and down the stairs, past the landlady who had been on her way to investigate the disturbance, and flung open the door.

'What on earth is going on?' she demanded.

The men were startled to have found her so easily, and so unaware of the trouble she had caused.

'You must come home, Princess. The King is concerned for your safety.'

'What nonsense,' Raina scoffed. 'I am with a friend, waiting for another. I am in no danger.'

But still the man took her by the arm and marched her straight back to the palace.

In the meantime, the soldier was arrested for kidnapping the Princess and taken directly to the King for sentencing.

The King was shocked to see the upstanding young man he had dined with brought before him and flung to his knees like any common criminal.

'You have been charged with kidnapping my only daughter out of her bedchamber in the middle of the night. You, a man I thought could be trusted! What have you to say for yourself?' the King demanded.

The soldier licked his lips and considered his options. It wouldn't do to mention the tinderbox, he thought, for summoning the Princess by magic was no different to taking her by physical force. Perhaps then he would be better off bending the truth a little.

'Your Highness, I meant your daughter no harm. I am lucky enough to have rooms just across the street, and happened to see from my window the Princess leaving the palace tonight. I am well aware that she is normally kept safe inside, so I was concerned, especially as she was unaccompanied. I invited her inside to look after her, Your Highness.'

The King grunted into his thick beard and folded his arms.

'And why not return her safely to the palace?'

'I would have, in time, but…forgive me, Your Highness, but the Princess seemed a little out of sorts. Having left the palace of her own accord, I thought perhaps she might become difficult if I suggested that she return, and I did not want to offend her enough that she refused my protection and went again into the night, alone.'

The soldier held his breath and kept his head bowed while the King took time to make up his mind.

'You may have been foolish,' said the King eventually, 'but I believe you acted with my daughter's best interests in mind. You are pardoned.'

The soldier let out a sigh, and sneaked a glance at the King to see if he might offer the final part of his story. The King indeed looked stern, but there was a fondness in his eyes as he looked down at the soldier.

'Your Highness,' he tried, for he had nothing to lose and everything to gain. 'Though I spent but a short while with the Princess, I must declare her the most charming thing I have ever known. I hope it does not offend Your Highness, but I believe I have fallen quite in love, and I flatter myself that she feels something of the same for me.'

*

Shut up once more in her room, Raina waited. She had been doing altogether too much waiting of late, she thought. And she feared for Betha, for the man with her tinderbox would not speak of her and she had begun to very much doubt that he had acquired the box fairly.

'How I wish you were here, Betha,' she said aloud, for she was so lonely in that room. 'If only I could summon you to me. If only you were still in this town. If only, dear Betha, you could help me.'

There was a breeze from the fireplace, and the burnt silvery ashes shifted and swirled and built themselves into a woman.

'Have I not always said, sweetheart, that all you need do is call?'

Betha's embrace was warm and strong, and Raina had no desire to resist it.

'That is not possible,' she whispered into Betha's soft neck.

'Why should it not be? I can make many things possible.'

Raina found with her lips something rough on Betha's flesh and opened her eyes, thinking that she might see a string or necklace of some kind, but what she saw instead was a puckered scar that wrapped all the way around, strangling her love. She followed it with her fingertips. Though she was not sure it was a story she wished to hear, she asked,

'What happened to you?'

'A soldier cut off my head, my sweet, and ran off with my tinderbox. But have no fear. I am healed, and I gave him back some memories while he went on his little treasure hunt.'

For a time Betha spoke more of what had happened between her and the soldier by the hollow tree, until quite unexpectedly Raina's maid burst in.

'My Lady, the King requests your presence immediately.'

She stopped short at the sight of Betha.

'You!' she gasped. 'You were not to return, on pain of death!'

'We shall talk to my father about that,' said Raina, and she took Betha's hand and led her to the King. 'Keep your head bowed,' she whispered, 'and stay behind me.'

As soon as they entered the King's presence, Betha did as she was told and nobody paid her any mind, thinking her to be one of the Princess's maids.

'You wished to see me, Father.'

The King beamed down from his throne at his daughter, his Queen seated beside him and the soldier standing before them both, facing Raina.

'You know I have feared for your future, my dear, since the prophecy was made. But we shall fear no more! This fine young gentleman has told me of his affection for you, and you for him, and has asked for your hand.'

The soldier smiled at her and reached for her hand.

'Our courtship may have been swift, my love, but – '

'Courtship?' asked the Princess.

'Worry not, dear Princess,' said the solder. 'We have nothing to hide. I have told the King how you took shelter with me tonight, how we spent those long hours in conversation, how we fell so quickly and so deeply for each other.'

Raina looked deep into the soldier's eyes and, to her great surprise, saw no deceit there.

'Is that how the night was for you?' asked she, and the soldier's confusion was clear. 'I believe we had differing experiences, Sir. And I am glad I grew no strong affection for you in our brief time together, for I have learned the most disturbing things about you.'

It was then that she stepped aside and revealed Betha, who raised her eyes to meet the soldier's.

'Impossible!' he gasped. 'You cannot be here!'

Betha smiled her pretty smile, lifted her arms and summoned again the spirits he had met in the cavern beneath the tree.

'You witch!' the soldier cried as the little girl, the shadows in the fog, and the young man who had once loved him advanced. One by one, each spirit told the King of the suffering that had befallen them thanks to the soldier, and with each word the soldier took another step away.

'For the crimes you have committed against these souls,' bellowed the King, 'I sentence you, false lord, to death.'

But before the King's men could restrain the soldier, he bolted. The spirits chased him from the palace, from the town, far away, and what they did when they caught him we shall never know, but he was certainly never seen again.

'And you, witch!' the King said, turning to Betha. 'Were you not banned for eternity from this town, for your prophecy of misfortune?'

Ashamed at their loss of the soldier, the King's men advanced quickly upon Betha, determined not to let two prisoners run free in one day.

But Betha tipped back her head, her silver hair glistening, and laughed.

'I may be a witch,' said she, 'but that was no magical prophecy.'

Raina took the hand of her lover and stepped bravely up to the King.

'She prophesised that I would love a commoner because I had already fallen for one.'

The King looked from the witch to the Princess, to his wife, to his men.

'This cannot be allowed. A Princess marry a witch? Such a thing would bring ridicule upon the whole kingdom.'

'Perhaps,' said Betha. 'Or perhaps it would bring respect, for I have great powers that many other kingdoms would envy.'

The King faltered, and turned to his daughter.

'My life cannot continue in this way, Father,' she said softly. 'What future do you see for me if you keep me shut away? Will you wait until my youth begins to wane, then marry me to a lord of your choosing and see me miserable? Or,' and she shifted her body closer to Betha, closing the space between them, 'would you rather your daughter lived happily, loved by her love, until her dying day?'

And so it was that the following week the King married his daughter to a witch, and the Kingdom rejoiced at the happy union.

## MOONSHINE'S WATERY BEAMS

When Tsukiko was young, her mother would hold her up to the sky at night and tell her,

'The Moon may look insubstantial from here, but she is great and powerful, and she will always guide you when you need her.'

Tsukiko grew happily to the cusp of adulthood, until one day her mother told her,

'I won't be around to look after you for much longer, little one. I am dying. But when I am gone, remember that you are not alone. Who will guide you?'

'The Moon,' said Tsukiko.

By the winter, her mother's grave was filled.

Her father wanted a new wife, a new mother for his daughter, and within a year he had married again. The stepmother was not kind to Tsukiko. She was a jealous woman.

Tsukiko was a hard worker and the stepmother was lazy, so she demanded all of Tsukiko's earned money for the household and left her none of her own to spend. But Tsukiko didn't desire a great many material things, so though the injustice infuriated her she did not suffer without her money.

Tsukiko was a pretty young woman, so the stepmother sent her outside as much as possible, hoping that the sun would damage her skin. But Tsukiko only grew more beautiful as the sun darkened her golden face.

Then the stepmother demanded to be called Mother, even though she knew that Tsukiko's heart was still raw from the loss of her real mother. This was something Tsukiko could not bear. It hurt her greatly, and she refused.

Not long after his marriage, Tsukiko's father was called away for business. He left his daughter, despite her objections, in the care of her stepmother. As soon as he had left the country, the stepmother moved with Tsukiko to a house on the edge of a forest, a forest that was said to be home to a witch.

One night, when the Moon was full, the stepmother took care to dampen every fire log and bury every candle in the garden so that they could not light the house, and then she cried to Tsukiko,

'We have no light! How are we to do anything in these conditions?'

Tsukiko, who had been sewing before the sun went down, moved her chair closer to the window to see by Moonlight.

'It is quite bright enough tonight,' she told the stepmother.

'But where have the candles gone? Perhaps whoever robbed us of light did so to come back later and rob us of more under the cloak of night!'

Knowing full well that her stepmother had hidden the candles somewhere, Tsukiko continued with her sewing and told her calmly,

'Tomorrow I shall go out and buy us some more candles.'

'No, no, that won't do,' the stepmother insisted. 'You might be content to strain your eyes, but I will not mistreat myself. You must go into the woods and ask the witch for light.'

'I hardly think that's necessary,' said Tsukiko. 'We can manage for one night. Go to bed early if you can't see to do anything.'

But the stepmother threw such a tantrum that Tsukiko, rolling her eyes at the woman's temper, put aside her needle and thread and fetched her coat.

There was no path through the forest, but she felt no fear. She looked up at the bright Moon and asked,

'How do I find the witch who lives here?'

The Moon's surface rippled and spilled over, sending a thin waterfall of light down into the forest. Tsukiko fixed her eyes on the beam and walked.

Many hours passed and her feet began to tire, but she kept on. She did not care whether her stepmother had light or not in the midnight hours, but her fascination was held by the Moonbeam that had answered her. Closer and closer it grew, and Tsukiko heard the sound of hurried feet in the undergrowth. An unclothed woman, her skin a deep indigo, ran past her, and with her she dragged the first half-light of dawn.

Still Tsukiko walked, and soon another woman ran past, a fiery red woman with a rope over her shoulder tugging the sun behind her.

The Moonbeam was almost invisible now, as the sun's light strengthened and took over, but Tsukiko was too close to give up.

Then she saw ahead of her a small hut, and sitting on the step was a woman whose skin was the colour of midnight and whose hair was a haze of white haloing her head. One eye looked much like anyone's eye, save that the iris was black, but the other was a pearly orb.

'Good morning,' said the midnight woman.

'Are you the witch?' Tsukiko asked.

'Some call me that.'

'And what shall I call you?'

'Hikari.'

'Good morning, Hikari. I am Tsukiko.'

'And what can I do for you, Tsukiko?'

'I have come for a light for my stepmother.'

Hikari held her palms up to the sky and laughed. Her laugh was a beautiful sound, a sound of hooting owls and trickling streams and quiet walks while the rest of the world sleeps. Tsukiko found herself just as drawn to the laugh as she had been to the Moonbeam. She sat down by Hikari on the step of the hut.

'What do you need in return for the light?' she asked.

Hikari fixed her mismatched stare on Tsukiko's sun-browned face and thought.

'Perhaps you would trade company.'

'Company?'

'Yes. Stay with me here, perhaps do some chores for me, and then I will give you a light for your stepmother.'

'Very well.'

Hikari leaned back against the hut door and stretched out her legs. The colour of her skin looked all the more rich for the simple white dress she wore. Tsukiko watched the toes curl in the early morning sunlight. She looked at the smooth arch of her feet and the curve of her calves.

'What would you do,' Hikari asked, 'if I asked you to bring me the dawn for breakfast?'

Tsukiko looked at the horizon. The sun was fully above it now, and even if it were early enough she would not know how to collect the dawn, or what part of it was edible.

'Perhaps a walk will help you think,' Hikari suggested. 'Although you have been walking for some time, haven't you? Maybe you passed the dawn on your way.'

Tsukiko got to her sore feet and walked back the way she had come, though without a guiding Moonbeam she could not be sure of the way. High in the sky, the pale daytime Moon was visible, so she asked of it,

'Where will I find the dawn?'

The Moon's surface rippled, and down again she sent a beam, though this time it was a thin wisp against the pale blue.

Tsukiko was glad to see that it was close, and she followed its lead until she came across a clearing in the woods where the indigo woman she had seen was touching her fingertips to blades of grass to melt the frost.

She cleared her throat.

'Good morning. I am Tsukiko. I have been sent by Hikari to invite you to breakfast with her.'

The woman smiled. Her nose and lips were dappled with dewdrops. She inclined her head briefly and followed Tsukiko back to Hikari's hut.

The smell of hot soup and steaming rice made Tsukiko think of her mother cooking when she was small. Outside the hut, Hikari was cooking fish on an open grill. She beamed to see the women approaching.

'That was quicker than I expected,' she said. 'I had hoped breakfast would be ready by the time you arrived.'

Then she fluttered her hands at the dawn and made soft sounds that Tsukiko presumed were words, though they sounded like no language she had ever heard. The dawn made no sound, but with a shift of the spine and a tap of a heel she replied. Tsukiko watched Hikari read the dawn's body and reply with motions of her own. Every gesture of her wrist was a wave across a sheet of satin, every move of her waist an ocean swell, every expression a subtle change in the light.

As they ate, Hikari translated and told Tsukiko of the dawn's work. In winter she had to melt the night ice, as Tsukiko had seen her doing. In the summer she left dew on the grass with her toes as she ran. She sang to wake the birds, and her touch on the earth sent the underground insects to sleep.

Tsukiko tried to keep her eyes on the dawn, for these were her words after all, but her gaze kept drifting back to Hikari and her pearly eye.

When they had finished their meal, the dawn took her leave.

'What other chores have you for me?' Tsukiko asked.

Hikari lay down in the grass and looked up at the cold sun.

'The sun seems so far away at this time of year,' she sighed. 'It's nice to see it close up in the day.'

This time Tsukiko knew exactly who she was looking for.

'Is the day close enough for me to find?' she asked the Moon, and waited for its beam.

The sun was higher now, and all she could see was a thin cord that disappeared unless the light hit it in the right way. But she saw it fall just beyond the clearing in which Hikari had built her hut.

Eager to please, Tsukiko ran this time.

The red woman was staring straight up, holding fast to a thick rope and guiding the flaming globe on its journey.

'Good morning. You must be the day. I am Tsukiko. Hikari would like you to visit.'

The woman smiled, and her hand made a gesture that Tsukiko did not know but took to be consent. The day altered her grip and followed Tsukiko, never once taking her eyes off her charge. Though she walked East, she managed to keep the fire drifting West.

Hikari leapt to her feet when she saw the day, and rushed over with the noises of flower petals unfurling, of hot stones, of fruit-heavy boughs. She did not mind that the day's eyes would not meet hers. Together they sat, and Hikari took Tsukiko's hand and pulled her down too. She tipped Tsukiko's chin to the sky, and the three of them sat and spoke of long days, short days, full days, soft days, any days that came into their minds.

Tsukiko tried to keep her eyes skywards like the others, but when Hikari opened her lips to speak in the gentle sounds of the day or to translate into familiar words for her, Tsukiko couldn't help but look away from the blue and the clouds and into the ink and the pearl.

When the day's rope grew taut, she had to leave. Her orb must keep on its endless journey, and she must guide it.

Hikari took Tsukiko inside her hut. The floor was covered with soft cushions and there was a window in the roof.

'I like to be able to see the sky,' said Hikari, 'even if I'm inside.'

They lay down together and watched the sky darken as the day took her light away.

'Have you any more chores for me?' Tsukiko asked.

'Just one more,' said Hikari, and her grinning teeth glowed against her skin. 'I would like you to brighten the midnight for me.'

Tsukiko reached out and touched the soft skin beneath Hikari's full moon eye.

'She is already bright,' she said.

'Then brighten her more.'

Tsukiko pressed her lips against the midnight's and ran her hands over her velvet body.

Hikari's halo of hair grew longer and brighter. The beam of her eye rested on her lover's heart.

'I have a light to send back to your stepmother,' she whispered. 'The light I reflect, the light that brightens me, the light that brought me the dawn and the day. Will you take it back to her?'

Tsukiko put her forehead to Hikari's forehead, her nose to her nose, her heart to her heart.

'No.'

## SPINNERS' LEGS

The Queen stood before her looking glass and smiled with rosy lips at the swollen globe of her belly.

'When my daughter is born to me,' she told her mirror, 'she will have hair as fine as silk and dark as coal. Her lips will be as red as blood, small and round and dainty as a cherry. When she opens them to sing, it will be the sweet chirp of a robin. When my daughter walks through the snow, it will be dull and grey against her skin. Snow White will be the fairest in the land.'

The Queen's reflection stretched its mouth in a wide smile and squinted, all teeth and no eyes, at the heavy belly.

'The last thing your daughter will be is fair.'

That night the Queen lay still in her bed. The white skin of her abdomen rippled gently outwards from her navel. She sighed and rolled over, cradling the lump of her daughter inside her. The gentle vibrations of a song shook her womb, a deep song, a rumbling song.

*

When the sun rose above the distant mountains, the Queen's belly was soft, not taut. She kneaded her flesh with both hands and looked around the room.

In the armchair by the window sat a young woman. Her black hair grew up and out from her head in tight, powerful coils. Her lips were thick, her nose broad, her shoulders wide. Her skin was dark as coal and when she opened her mouth to sing it was the roar of an avalanche.

'Who are you?'

76

The young woman smiled.

'I am yours, Mother. I am Snow White.'

The Queen had prepared a room for her daughter, filled with pretty trinkets and playthings to amuse a young Princess.

'Perhaps if you stay away from the sun you will become fairer,' she told her daughter. 'You must not let its rays darken your skin.'

But Snow White did not care for the things in her room. She spent her days in the fields tending to the horses, or in the woods with her bow, or singing to the mountains until parts of them crumbled off and tumbled down to meet her.

'Won't you stay inside today?' asked the Queen of her daughter. 'Won't you stitch flowers onto this tablecloth and talk to me?'

Snow White sat down with her mother, but she hadn't the patience for such work.

'This is too hard for me,' she said when she dropped the needle for the seventh time. 'I cannot keep this delicate thing between my fingers. I shall knap arrowheads while we talk.'

By the end of the day, Snow White had filled her quiver with new arrows.

In the room the Queen had prepared for her daughter, there was a small bird in a cage. It was a dainty blue thing whose song could not be heard over the sound of a dropped pin.

'Won't you learn to sing like your bird today?' asked the Queen. 'It is such a pretty song. A Princess should be able to sing a delicate song like that.'

Snow White shut herself up in her room for hours, and the Queen listened with tears of delight in her eyes to the gentle sound she made. When the song was so beautiful that she could stand it no more, the Queen flung open the door, full of praise for her daughter.

All the kind words froze on her tongue when she saw the room.

Clinging to every surface, draped over each chair, hanging in softly swaying tendrils from the ceiling, were infinite cobwebs. They gleamed in the evening light, thin cords of spun sugar coating the room. The thousand spiders wove their webs to the sweet song of Snow White. The bird cage was open and empty.

*

That night the Queen spoke once more to her mirror.

'How ever is my daughter to win the hearts of the people with skin and strength and a voice like hers? She is not the Princess I wished her to be.'

Her reflection opened its sharp-toothed mouth and laughed.

'She cannot win hearts until her heart has been won,' it said. 'When her heart is no longer her own, when she has been tamed, then the people will see her as the Princess you wanted.'

'How can anyone ever win her heart?'

The reflection licked its lips with a long blue tongue.

'Are you prepared to do whatever it takes?'

'For my daughter's future,' said the Queen, 'I must. What do I do?'

So the mirror told her.

\*

Snow White hunted alone. She crept through the tightly packed trees on the trail of a deer. Scattered leaves, turned earth, a splash of urine. She followed these signs deeper and deeper into the forest, listening to the spiders' weaving songs if she ever doubted her way. Soon she could see a small clearing ahead where the young doe nibbled the greenery while her ever twitching ears kept watch. She moved around a flat slab of stone to find the choicest clumps of grass. Snow White crept forward an inch at a time in her soft leather boots, closing in with all the patience of a born hunter.

A twig broke.

Snow White turned. Behind her stood her mother, knife raised.

'Mother?'

Her arrow was aimed at her mother's heart. She lowered the bow.

'If you wished me gone, I would gladly have left. You do not have to kill me, Mother. I shall be gone within the hour if it will make you happy.'

Her mother dropped the knife and fell to her knees.

'That was not my intention,' she sobbed. 'Not to kill you, my darling, never to kill you. But how ever will you win hearts when you are not the way a Princess should be? I only want the best for you, my sweet girl.'

Snow White knelt beside the Queen and held her in her arms.

'Do you not think I am worthy, my Lady? Do you not think I have skill and strength and cunning? Do you not think I have knowledge aplenty and beauty to top it all?'

The Queen wept for her daughter. She wept for the coal-black, spring-haired, broad-hipped, muscled girl who thought she was beautiful. For her daughter's own good, she must do as the mirror had told her. She opened the bag on her shoulder.

'Let us eat together, and forget.'

From her bag she took a purple cloth which she spread upon the stone slab in the clearing. It was large enough to drape prettily over the sides, making a noble dais of the stone. She placed upon it two rolls of bread, two small rounds of cheese, two bunches of grapes, and two shining red apples. Together they knelt and ate their meal. Snow White spoke of how the spiders loved her, how her aim was improving every day, how it was easier every time she had to carry a carcass back to the palace over her shoulders. The Queen listened and held back her tears. She bit into her crisp apple, clear juices running down her wrist from the bright white centre. Snow White picked up her apple too. She tossed it from hand to hand while she spoke, buffed it on her jacket, rolled it between her palms. The Queen sat, tense, watching.

Snow White sank her teeth into the crimson skin.

\*

Upon the dais lay the Princess, raised and on display as she should be. The Queen arranged her daughter's limbs so that she lay neatly on her back, arms folded over her abdomen, the way a sleeping Princess should lie. Now that her daughter was unarmed, she took up her dagger once more and sliced open Snow White's chest.

There lay her beating heart, glowing hot and full of power beneath her ribs.

Then the Queen left her, quite sure she would be safe, and made her way back to the palace.

'The deed is done,' she told her mirror.

Her reflection lurched towards her eagerly.

'And how was it done? Did you cut out her heart yourself?'

'I could not,' she confessed. 'I used the apple. She lies in the forest with her heart on display for any man who finds her.'

The reflection's smile stretched all the way up to the corners of its eyes.

'Then it is time for you to gather the people. The quicker someone takes her heart, the better.'

The Queen nodded and made the necessary preparations.

'The Princess lies in the forest,' she declared to the crowded hall from her throne that evening. 'Her heart waits to be claimed by whoever of you is brave enough to find her. You will need but a kiss to unlock her ribcage. With one kiss, her heart will be for the taking.'

\*

Deep in the forest, the spiders mourned. They spun their webs around the fallen hunter, cocooned her in silk, crawled into her chest and sat on her heart to keep it warm and alive. On thousands of spindly legs, they lifted her and scuttled through the undergrowth to find a hidden nook large enough to house her. Snow White's stiff body seemed to hover just above the earth as the spiders carried her. Birds were startled into flight at the sight of their curious burden. Rabbits leapt into bushes and deer bolted as the spiders and their Princess neared. Towards the shadows they moved, to all the places they knew best, but Snow White was not of a species small enough to squeeze into holes in trees, under logs, into piles of undisturbed leaves. They took her to a cool cave with a ceiling dripping stalactites, and there they laid her down.

\*

The woodcutter's son had a noble heart. When he heard gossip in the tavern of Snow White's fate and the Queen's promise, he determined to set out himself to find her. He went on foot with a sword in his hand and a knife in his belt, and hid behind a tree to watch the knights gather with the sons of lords and earls to ride out into the woods for the Princess. He watched them slap each other's backs and laugh broadly at suggestions of what pleasures they might enjoy once the Princess's heart was in their hands. What a novelty she was to them, with her strong body and fierce will.

'I know how to tame a bitch,' crowed one knight.

'I know how to make them beg,' said another.

'Why take the time?' asked one of the sons. 'No-one said we had to wake her as soon as we find her.'

The woodcutter's son watched them ride off together, hunting hounds at the heels of their horses to sniff the way.

'I will not treat you so foully, Snow White,' he whispered. 'As my wife, you will be respected. I will treasure you, honour you, and love you. I know how to look after a lady's heart.'

He set off alone, ignoring the trail the horses had made. He knew of the stone slab in the clearing, and he had heard people talk of how she lay on a stone table somewhere in the woods. It took him over an hour, but the young man found the clearing just where he knew it was. There was the cloth, spread out without a crease, but no Princess slept upon it.

The woodcutter's son sat down and wept for the girl who had surely been taken by the other men.

A spider crawled over his boot.

\*

Above the Princess, a droplet of water crawled down a stalactite. It clung to the tip for a moment as though it longed to stay safely above the world, tethered to the bones of its ancestors. Then it stretched and broke away, a tiny sphere of water falling through the cold air until it broke upon the lips of Snow White.

Her eyes opened.

The woodcutter's son's footsteps could be heard, approaching slowly across the stone and echoing around the cavern.

'Princess?'

He knelt beside her and looked into her chest. Her heart was black and furry, a repulsive ball convulsing inside her. The man shuddered.

'I shall clean your heart when I take it out,' he told her. 'Then I will look after it, tend to it for the rest of my days, and you will be a true Princess.'

He leaned down bravely, ignoring the revolting growth in her chest, to touch his lips to hers.

Snow White's hand shot up and clasped his throat.

'My heart is just fine.'

She sat up, keeping him an arm's length away from her, his lips pursed uselessly, his eyes wide with shock.

'I have creatures far better than you taking care of it.'

The spiders scuttled out from every corner, every hole, every crack in the stone. The guardians of her heart left the warm, pulsing muscle to join their kin. They covered the young man's legs, a great blanket of writhing black wires, and held him down. Snow White rose to her feet and looked down at the boy.

'What monster are you?' he gasped. 'To have these beasts under your control! It is the work of a demon!'

Snow White laughed, a great lively boom that shook the cave and would have filled his ears even without the accompaniment of echoes.

'Is that how much you fear me, boy? That you must call me a demon, a witch, an evil beast? Is that all that you think has the power to terrify you?'

81

She sang then, with the sweet voice the spiders loved, and asked them to let him be.

'He is no threat to us,' she told them in her song. 'See how he trembles in our presence.'

The swarm receded.

'Please tell my mother that I will be back,' said Snow White to the woodcutter's son.

Then she lay back on the floor beneath the stalactites, and let the cave's kisses stitch her skin back together.

\*

The Queen was busy with her embroidery when Snow White returned. There was no knock, only the sound of the door slamming against the wall when Snow White threw it open.

'I am not fair game.'

The Queen's needle dropped from her fingers.

'My darling!' she cried, rushing towards her daughter. 'Who has your heart?'

'I have my heart, Mother. And I will always have my heart, for it is mine and mine alone.'

The Queen's face fell. She turned to her mirror desperately.

'Help me! She has outwitted us somehow. What am I to do?'

Her reflection stepped close to the glass and its face split open in its wide, toothy grin.

'What I have always said,' it told her. 'You must cut out her heart yourself, offer it up yourself. She cannot keep it a moment longer. She is too strong when she has control of herself.'

The Queen turned back to her daughter to find an arrow pointing straight at her. Snow White's elbow was raised high, drawing the string back tightly.

'Please, my darling,' begged the Queen. 'Let me do this. However will anyone love you if you do not let me help you?'

Snow White loosed an arrow into her mother's heart.

For her coronation, the palace was decorated with the silk of spiders.

# LAZY FINGER

When the Emperor of a great and powerful land died, he left behind him an Empress and a daughter. Determined that the empire should not fall without her husband, the Empress offered her daughter to the son of a neighbouring Emperor. Within days the arrangements were made, and the Princess was sent off on horseback to wed the Prince.

A great many jewels, silks and other fine trinkets were loaded onto the Princess's horse before she left, and she was dressed in a fine gown embroidered all over with silver thread. A handmaiden named Falada was sent to accompany the Princess on her journey.

Now, the Princess had no desire to be married to a man she had never met, and fearing that she would detest the Prince she stopped her horse by a river and dismounted.

'Dear Falada, how I wish I had more time to fall in love,' the poor Princess cried. 'And yet I wish to honour my father, and obey my mother. Whatever shall I do, my dear?'

The Princess took a long drink from the river.

'Why don't you drink too, sweet Falada? We have such a ride ahead of us.'

The Princess mounted the horse and waited. When Falada had quenched her thirst, she made to climb back upon her horse.

'My Lady, I believe you have taken my horse.'

The Princess laughed.

'How silly of me! But a horse is a horse, my dear. You take mine and let us be on our way.'

They rode on, Falada now with the heavy bags of treasure behind her calves.

Some time later, the Princess stopped at a pond.

'Ah! How thirsty I am again. Falada, it is time we took another rest.'

The Princess bent over the pool to drink, but her hair fell over her face.

'Lend me your scarf, my dear, that I might bind back my hair to drink.'

Falada removed the old linen scarf from her head, releasing her own ink-black sheet of hair, and helped the Princess to tie up her locks. The Princess bent and drank with no more trouble, then hopped back up onto her horse and waited for her maid to drink.

On they rode once more. Falada's hair streamed behind her in the wind and the treasure bags pounded at the flanks of her galloping horse.

A mile from the gates of her fiancé's city, the Princess stopped again by a waterfall.

'We have been riding for so long,' she said. 'I am weary. Perhaps a shock of cold water will help revive me. And I must be clean before I present myself to my Prince.'

The Princess plunged herself into the pool.

'Ah! I feel better already!'

She swam to the shore and stepped out again.

'How silly of me. My dress is soaked through!'

She stripped off the silk gown and stepped under the waterfall once more, rubbing the dirt of the journey from her skin.

'Falada, my dear,' she called. 'I cannot arrive in a sodden gown! It is not proper, and besides, I shall catch my death wearing that now. I shall take your dress, and you shall put on mine.'

'Yes, my Lady.'

Falada took off her dress.

'And you may as well bathe before you dress. After all, it is such a pretty gown. Let us put a clean, pretty girl in it.'

So Falada bathed and dressed in the Princess's clothes, and the Princess dressed in her faithful servant's bone dry woollen skirt and bodice.

When the Princess and Falada rode up to the gate, the Emperor was waiting to personally greet them. Seeing the sodden state of Falada's gown, her rushed to her, helped her from her horse, and begged her to tell him what harm had befallen her on the journey. Falada, nervous of speaking to an Emperor, turned to the Princess to let her explain.

'If I may, Your Highness,' said the Princess with a bow. 'My mistress is tired after our troubles. A gang of thieves tried to stop us on the road, and she was thrown from her horse into the river. I praise the fates that we are alive and well, my Lord.'

Thinking Falada sorely shaken and a delicate, shy princess, the Emperor passed her hand to one of his wife's own maids and ordered her to be given all the comforts the palace had to offer.

'I'm sure your mistress will reward your loyalty and service,' the Emperor said to the Princess. 'Now, go about your duties. The maids will show you where to take your mistress' things.'

Later that evening, when a bath had been drawn for Falada, sprinkled with rose petals and scented with salts, the Princess told the other maids,

'My mistress is shy and far from home. Please allow me to wait on her alone.'

Falada lay submerged in the warm water and waited for her orders. The Princess knelt beside the tub.

'You are the Princess now, my dear. You will not tell a single soul who you really are, or I shall cut off your head myself. If we do not like this Prince, you shall be married to him. If we do like him, I shall tell them all how you stole my clothes and horse and treasures on the road and forced me to act as your maid. And then I shall marry him.'

'My Lady!' cried Falada. 'How could you tell such lies?'

'Easily, my dear, so easily. And they will believe me. Just look at your hands.'

She took one of Falada's rough little hands in her soft palm.

'Your own body will speak against you.'

So it was that Falada was left to be courted by the Prince, and the Princess to work as her maid. One day, having been forced to wash gowns to keep up the appearance of a maid, the Princess collapsed on Falada's bed and cried,

'This work is too hard for me, my dear. You must find me something easier to do. Tell the Emperor I am loyal and hardworking, and that I deserve easier work to reward me.'

Still scared for her head, Falada went to speak with the Emperor.

'I would like different work for my maid.'

The Emperor was confused.

'But why? Is she not loyal? Has she not accompanied you far from home, leaving her own family behind to stay by your side?'

Falada thought then of her family. She thought of her mother and father, who had both toiled all their lives to provide for her and her sister. She thought of her home, and of all she would lose if she married the Prince and played the Princess for the rest of her life.

'She is lazy and incompetent,' Falada told the Emperor. 'Her mother was once loyal and true to mine, but has now passed on. I could not bear to let the girl go, for the sake of her mother's memory, but she is fit for only the simplest, easiest work.'

The Emperor felt sorry for the sweet young Princess whose kind heart led her to put up with such a useless servant. He thought long and hard, and finally decided that the maid should be put to work assisting the goose girl.

The next morning, the Princess met the goose girl, whose name was Curdkena.

'I'm sure it will be such fun to work with you,' said the Princess, eyes a-flutter, to the goose girl. 'What is our job?'

'Every morning we drive the geese into the meadows to feed, and every evening we drive them back to their coop,' said Curdkena. 'It is simple work, but lonely. Your company will be a blessing.'

The Princess followed Curdkena and the geese to the meadow, chattering all the while until she was sure the goose girl liked her.

'Curdkena, my sweet,' she said when they arrived in the meadow. 'My feet are not used to such walking. I must rest a while.'

The Princess sat down to rest. As she sat, she unbound her hair and began to comb the fine, dark locks until they shone. As she combed she sang to herself.

'Falada, Falada, how dost thou fare?

Trapped with thy Prince while I tend to my hair.

I think of my mother, oh, if she knew it,

Sadly, sadly, she would rue it!'

The Princess combed her hair and sang until the sun began to set and Curdkena drove the geese back to the city.

The next day was much the same, with Curdkena never taking her eyes from her charges while the Princess combed and sang without a care in the world.

One evening, when the goose girl had shut the geese up for the night and was making her way home to bed, she met Falada.

86

'My Lady,' she said with a curtesy, taking her for the Princess she pretended to be.

'You must be the girl my maid was sent to work with. How does she manage?' asked Falada.

'My Lady, the truth is not what you must hope. She does naught but comb her hair all day while I mind the geese. And over and over she sings the same song.'

'What is it she sings?'

So the goose girl sang the Princess's gloating song.

'Falada, Falada, how dost thou fare?

Trapped with thy Prince while I tend to my hair.

I think of my mother, oh, if she knew it,

Sadly, sadly, she would rue it!'

Falada took Curdkena by the shoulders and kissed each of her cheeks.

'You have done well to tell me,' she said. 'You will be rid of her soon.'

Falada returned to the palace to speak with the Emperor.

'Curdkena, the poor goose girl, has complained that my maid does nothing of even the simple job you have given her. I cannot believe that even my lazy maid could be quite so useless, and yet the girl seemed so sincere. I wish for us to witness my maid in her work.'

The Emperor, whose heart had quickly softened to the sweet young Princess who was to be his daughter, agreed in an instant.

The next morning, the Emperor and Falada waited in the shadows of the city gates for the goose girl and the Princess to pass, and followed them all the way to the meadow. There they saw the Princess sit on the grass and comb out her hair and sing her strange song. When they had seen enough, they returned to the palace.

'What a curious rhyme,' said the Emperor. 'I have never heard it before. Who is this Falada?'

'I cannot say, my Lord,' said Falada, her eyes wide with innocence. 'Perhaps we should ask her to explain herself.'

When the Princess returned to the palace that evening to see Falada, the Emperor was waiting for her.

'Explain yourself, girl!'

The Princess trembled under his gaze, fearing that Falada had told all.

'She has told you lies, Your Highness! She threatened to kill me if I revealed myself to be the true Princess! She wanted the Prince, the money, everything for herself!'

Behind the Emperor, Falada smiled, for she knew that of course the Emperor had been about to ask only about the Princess's work. Now, he sat down heavily and looked from the Princess to Falada and back again. Falada sang.

> 'Falada, Falada, how dost thou fare?
> Trapped with thy Prince while I tend to my hair.
> I think of my mother, oh, if she knew it,
> Sadly, sadly, she would rue it.'

The true Princess burst into tears, feeling herself cornered. She confessed everything while Falada stood silent, her head safe and sound.

The Emperor, furious with the Princess for her deception, refused to marry the girl to his son and instead sent her, her treasures, and her shame back to her mother. As for Falada, he was still fond of her and pitied her plight. Convinced that a girl who had so successfully been disguised as a princess would surely make an excellent wife for his son, the Emperor offered Falada the marriage she had been preparing for.

'You are too kind, my Lord,' she said with a curtesy, 'but I fear the life of a princess is not for me. But if you would be so good, I'm sure my family would be excellent subjects. If a home could be made for them here, I would be forever grateful.'

The Emperor immediately had a charming cottage prepared for Falada's family, and gave her work with the goose girl.

Now Falada and Curdkena herd geese from the city to the meadow and back day by day, Falada busy with work she enjoys and Curdkena happy with the company she has always longed for.

## Not So Big

There was once a young man who met a young woman and fell in love, as young people are wont to do. The couple were married, and within two years the woman had given birth to a healthy pair of twins whom she named Isobel and Isaac.

While his family grew, the man began to trade. He found he was rather good at obtaining things for a low price and selling them for a substantial profit, so he traded more goods from further away with more people, and so his wealth grew.

His wife would have been greatly pleased by this, for wealth makes many things in life easier, but her husband began to neglect the children and herself. She was forced to give up her job as a farm worker, for her husband had no time to look after the children while she worked, and he made far more money than she.

The wife loved her husband still, but she felt him drawing further and further from the family as his fortune grew and grew. She loved her children, but they exhausted her when she had to cope alone.

Eventually the day came when the husband returned home from a long trip abroad, and the wife said,

'I love you, but I cannot go on like this.'

'Like what?' asked the husband. 'We've nearly saved enough money to move to a bigger house.'

'We have moved five times in three years,' said the wife. She wanted to shout, but the children were asleep. 'Money is lovely. Money gets us food, and a home, and toys for the children. But it doesn't give us time.'

The husband laughed forcefully, for he did not understand and he wanted the fight to end.

'Nothing can give us more time, darling, but money can buy us quality time.'

'Can it? The children barely see you. I barely see you. Are we a family, or aren't we?'

So it was decided that they would not be.

The wife took back her old job at the farm. There she could work and keep an eye on the children as they played in the fields and barns around her. She bought a little house of her own and did well for herself for some time, but as the children grew and their appetites grew, she found herself stretched.

'I love you terribly, Isobel and Isaac,' she said to her little ones. 'But you may have to live with your father for a while. He has more money than I, and will be able to give you more.'

She hated herself for saying it, for teaching her babies that more money meant better care.

The husband, meanwhile, had been away and back again several times, each time bringing home more goods for his clients and more money for himself. When he arrived at his house, which was really very large and had suites enough for ten people to stay, he was surprised to see his wife with two young children he hardly recognised.

'Why don't you go and explore Daddy's house?' she told the children, and sent them running off down the long hallways.

The husband took her into a drawing room and called for someone to bring them tea.

'The children have grown,' he said, and until he saw her reaction he was not even sure they were his children. How old would they be now? Four? Six? He wasn't sure.

'I can't provide for the children. The more they grow, the more they need. I want a tutor for them, to teach them to read and write better than I do. I want them to have more than one set of clothes, but with my money I struggle just to keep up with replacing all the worn out, tiny clothes...'

The husband nodded solemnly as she told him her woes, and he poured the tea and passed her sandwiches and cakes finer and more plentiful than the food she would have had for her evening meal.

Finally, the wife came to the question she had come to ask, though it hurt her to do it.

'Can the children live with you?'

The husband choked on a mouthful of fruit cake.

'With me? Oh no, I don't think that would do.'

'They are your children,' she reasoned.

'I've had nothing to do with them for...'

He was not sure for how long.

'Precisely,' said the wife. 'Wouldn't you like the chance to bond with them? It wouldn't be for ever. I can work more without them, save up a little, and then I'll be able to take them back.'

The husband thought about how two small children would fit into his life. It seemed a rather huge task. After some time, he suggested a compromise. It took much convincing, for the wife would not be able to build up her savings quite as soon, but as the husband would not take both children she had no choice. It broke her heart, but in the end the wife agreed to split Isaac and Isobel apart.

The husband sat both children down in front of him, all wild hair and pink cheeks and skinny legs sticking out of short trousers. He considered them.

A boy he would be expected to teach, to train as an apprentice and prepare to take over the business when he retired. Useful though that may be, he did not relish the idea of such close contact with the child, day in, day out, for ever.

A girl he might get away with not training. He could take her to meet his clients, take her to parties with his friends, have her dressed up nicely as a sweet accessory. And when she was older, he was sure he could arrange a marriage that would benefit himself.

'I'll take the girl, then,' he said.

When Isaac and Isobel realised what was happening, they clung to each other and shrieked. Isaac tried to push his father away from his sister. Isobel tried to bite his hand when he brushed her brother aside. They screamed in perfect harmony, as loud and long as each other, and their mother's heart tore itself in two.

In the darkness of midnight, on the first day of their lives that they had been apart, Isobel and Isaac met in each other's dreams.

*

When Isobel was a young woman, her father's many wealthy friends began to talk to her differently. Many of them at one time or another said to her,

'You are so beautiful, Belle. Your mother must have been a prophetess to name you so perfectly.'

91

'My name is not Belle,' she told every one. 'My name is Isobel.'

One day her father decided to throw a great masked ball for all his friends, and so Isobel found herself once again among endless wealthy acquaintances all vying for her attentions and trying to flatter her with a nickname she did not desire. She tired of this quickly and, behind her feathered mask, took herself off to a quiet courtyard at the centre of her father's mansion. She tried to send herself into the waking dreams in which she spoke to Isaac, but the tranquillity of the night was disturbed by an unfamiliar voice.

'Good evening. You must be Isobel.'

'Must I?'

'If you like to be,' said the voice.

'And if I do not?'

'Then you are not. But if that is the case, I would very much like to have a name by which I may call you.'

Isobel turned around and saw someone in a magnificent golden coat and breeches, with a huge mask covered in fine fur.

'You may call me Issy,' she said on a whim, for she liked his decadent disguise. 'But never Belle.'

'And you may call me Leo.' She heard the smile in his voice, though she could not see his face. 'But never Nardo.'

She laughed and held his hand in hers for a moment.

'It is a pleasure to meet you, Leo.'

*

The ocean is not a safe place. Isobel's father had been lucky for many years, but luck cannot last for ever. One by one his ships were lost. Some were wrecked in vicious storms, some were taken by pirates, some seemed to disappear off the Earth's very face and were never seen again. He was greatly disturbed by this, but he had counted that he had enough wealth left to sustain himself and his daughter for three full years while he built his business up again.

Isobel and her father continued to live as they had done, until one day they returned from a social visit to find their home burned to the ground, and everything in it.

'How can this be?' cried Isobel's father. 'Everything I owned was in that house! We have not a penny left in the world!'

The hills around called his words back to him, and before they had quieted somebody else spoke.

'If Isobel chooses to live with me, I can give you all the wealth you desire for yourself. Would you like that?'

He wore a different coat, this one the colour of fine red wine, but the fur mask still covered his face.

Isobel's father thought of the home he had lost, and then thought of a home even bigger and better.

'Is there no limit to your wealth, sir?' he asked.

'None at all,' said Leo. 'All I ask is your daughter's company. And she must be willing.'

'And if I am not?' asked Isobel.

'Then you shall not come.'

Isobel saw his mane then for what it truly was. His nose was wide and flat, his upper lip hung loosely over his lower, his eyes were a little further apart than she had been taught to draw them.

'Very well,' said Isobel. 'I'll go with you, and Father can have his money.'

So the three set off together to Leo's home, which turned out to be a castle with large grounds surrounding it and many hidden courtyards. The doors seemed endlessly tall, and the ceiling of the entrance hall was higher than the roof of Isobel's father's house had been.

Leo strode through the castle, flinging open door after door to expose rooms filled with grand statues, antique instruments, jewels, chests of gold.

'Take what you will,' he said to Isobel's father, and he opened up an empty chest in one room. 'Fill this with whatever you desire, and it will be sent with you to new lodgings that will be yours until you have built another home for yourself.'

Isobel's father immediately began to grab all the most expensive looking jewellery, then the slightly less impressive pieces, then all the rest and still the chest was not even a quarter full. He heaved into it huge marble carvings which looked bigger than the chest itself, and yet once they were inside there was still more room. Only when his arms ached and he wished for nothing more than a hot meal and a bed did the chest finally look full. He closed it, thanked Leo and asked to be directed to his new lodgings.

'Lie down and close your eyes,' said Leo.

Isobel's father wondered for a moment if he were being made a fool of, but as he had been allowed to strip many of Leo's rooms bare he thought there was no harm in playing along. He lay down on the floor and closed his eyes.

Isobel watched her father disappear. He had not looked at her since he began looting Leo's rooms.

'Goodbye, Father,' she said to the empty air.

Leo cleared his throat with a low, rumbling growl.

'We shall dine together now, if that is agreeable.'

'And if it is not?'

'Then we shall not.'

Isobel took Leo's elbow and followed him to the dining room.

*

At the very moment that Isobel touched Leo's arm, Isaac's feet met the ground as he dismounted. He had, in the past few years, taken to late night rides around the countryside, though his mother discouraged it. Several young men of the farm had disappeared – to seek their fortune, to elope, lost in accidents, nobody knew – and she grew more concerned for her son with each passing day.

Isaac's favourite horse was one he had broken in himself, and it was she that he rode that night. She was a grey shire horse, sixteen hands high, and he had named her Issy. The human Issy had been delighted.

While Isaac was brushing down her coat, chatting idly to her as he always did, somebody else entered the stable.

'How would you like a little extra work?'

He turned to see a woman dressed far more finely than anyone who worked on the farm.

'I am Lady Gormain, and I require your services, farm boy.'

Isaac bowed to the woman, for he knew her to be the lady who owned the land that he farmed and a great deal more besides.

'It would be an honour to serve you, my Lady,' he said.

'Excellent,' said she, and her wide smile could have devoured him whole.

*

Things are not always as simple as they seem. Isobel and Isaac knew this, for others would have them believe that their dreams were just dreams, and yet they knew them to be more.

'I have gone to live with a beast,' Isobel told Isaac.

'How terrifying. I have gone to live with the Lady of the Manor,' Isaac told Isobel.

'How delightful.'

They sat together in a tree they had played in as children, a tree that had long since been eaten up with disease and removed from the world.

'What is it like?' they asked together, and laughed.

Isaac answered first.

'It is strange,' he said. 'I move things and fix things. I bring in deliveries. I never knew someone could own so much furniture and still want more.'

'And she lets a farm boy wander round her house at his leisure, does she?'

'Not quite. Every door in the place is locked, and she will only open one at a time for me. I imagine I haven't seen most of the house. It's hard to map it out in my mind when I only see it room by room.'

Then Isobel answered.

'It's quite lovely, really. He's kind. He cooks well. Or I suppose he does. We eat very nice meals, but I have never seen any staff.' She frowned. 'I have never seen him cook or set the table either, though.'

'The mark of a good servant is not being seen. Perhaps he simply has the best of the best.'

'With all the wealth he had to give away to Father, I shouldn't be surprised.'

'How is Father?' asked Isaac, because he thought he should.

'You don't care, and nor do I,' said Isobel. 'How is Mother?'

'Still unwell,' said Isaac. 'I do hope the summer perks her up.'

'Send her my love.'

'You know she never believes us.'

'Then I shall write an honest-to-goodness letter tomorrow, and you can read that to her.'

*

Isobel was quite content with her life. Her mind was kept busy with the books in Leo's library, the paintings that hung upon his walls, and the array of plants she had never seen before in his gardens.

'I think this day has the perfect weather for a walk outside, if you would care to join me,' Leo said to her one morning over breakfast.

Isobel smiled coyly at him.

'And if I would not?'

Leo's small eyes crinkled.

'Then you shall not.'

Arm in arm, they took the gravelled paths around the flower beds, and whenever Isobel did not recognise a flower Leo was able to tell her its name. After some time, she stepped off the path onto the lawn and led Leo towards the trees around the edge of the castle grounds.

'I do like your ornamental gardens,' she said, 'but there is something too contained about them.' She waved a hand at the trees. 'This is much more like home to me. The lands around the farm my mother and brother work on are wilder. The people there are too busy tending to crops and cattle to make pretty gardens.'

For a moment she felt sad for her mother who would not believe that Isaac spoke to her. She had written the letter she promised, and Isaac had read every word, but she knew her mother still worried every day that she did not see her daughter.

Leo tugged gently on her arm.

'There is a flower I would like you to see, Issy.'

He took her to an untended patch behind the trees, and there grew a plant with curious flowers. Tiny violet petals curled over and over, and in the centre was a long, pale point tipped with dark purple.

'Trachystemon orientalis,' said Leo, for he saw that she did not recognise the plant. 'Also known as Abraham-Isaac-Jacob.'

Isobel could have wept when Leo spoke her brother's name. Her dreams suddenly seemed so distant, and she longed to see him in her waking hours.

'You may visit your family, dear Issy, if you wish. I only ask that you return within one month, and that you return of your own free will.'

'And if I do not wish to return?'

There was a deep sadness in the smile Leo offered her in return. 'Then you will not.'

*

Isaac was quite content with his life. His hands were kept busy repairing bannisters, painting skirting boards, and moving Lady Gormain's new purchases from room to room, though she followed him all the way with her keys, locking doors behind him as soon as he had passed through.

'The time has come for me to trust you,' said Lady Gormain one morning. 'Though my hand has been forced; it is hardly a choice.'

She took from her belt the ring of keys for the house and held them out to Isaac.

'Here is every key for every lock,' she told him. 'I have been called away on urgent business, but I have an important delivery of paintings arriving today. Here is a list of what must be hung in which room. I expect it all to be done by the time I arrive home tomorrow evening.'

'Of course, my Lady,' said Isaac with his customary bow.

'You may use any key necessary. But this one,' and she held up the smallest, dullest key on the ring, 'you will never have to use, and must not.'

It happened that the day the Lady left was the day that Isobel arrived. She rode up to the house as the Lady rode away, and as soon as she saw Isaac standing at the door she leapt from her horse and they clung to each other, each overjoyed to be awake and together.

'I have brought you your flower self,' said Isobel, and presented him with a bunch of Abraham-Isaac-Jacob.

He laughed when she told him, and was sorry that he had nothing to give her.

'I would much rather have surprised you than had a gift,' said Isobel.

'How about I give you a tour of my stately home?' said Isaac, affecting the accent of Lady Gormain.

'What, of the one room you are allowed in today?'

Isaac jingled the ring of keys.

'I have special privileges today.'

So the two set about exploring the place, and Isaac finally began to see how each room connected. He told Isobel everything he knew of any objects of interest, mostly the origin of the furniture he had carried in.

A loud bell sounded through the empty house, and Isaac took Isobel to the front door to help him collect the delivery. Many more huge gilt frames than he had expected had arrived, and some he and Isobel could barely lift together.

'What an extravagant woman, to have so many new things so often,' said Isobel.

'Does your Leo not spend his money as lavishly?'

'Not at all. His castle is very grand, of course, but since I arrived I have seen no evidence of him spending anything at all.'

'I can't decide what is stranger,' said Isaac with a laugh. 'To throw one's money around without a single care, or to hoard it all in a dusty pile.'

It took the whole of the day for the twins to move each painting, one by one, to its new home, and to hang it where Lady Gormain's list instructed. It was not until the last one was on the wall that Isaac remembered the littlest key and told Isobel.

'How strange,' she said. 'Shall we try to find what it opens?'

They set about fitting the key into chests and cupboards and dressers and drawers and any number of small locks on small things, but the key fit none of them, and eventually they tired.

'Did you see Mother before you came here?' Isaac asked, and since Isobel had not and their work was done, they set off home.

There is little more to be said of Isobel's visit. She worked with her mother while Isaac worked for the Lady, and when all was finished they spent long hours as the family they used to be. Isaac and Isobel visited their childhood hideouts; they took their mother, whose health had greatly improved, for long walks in the sunshine; they bathed in streams and took small picnic dinners out into the evening.

On the very last day of Isobel's visit, Lady Gormain once again handed the ring of keys over to Isaac. She sniffed haughtily, quite unhappy about it.

'I suppose you proved yourself trustworthy last time. I have only a few pieces arriving today, so you will need fewer keys than you needed before. And you will not,' she held up the small one, 'need this one.'

Isobel, meanwhile, was upset. Every second with her family had been perfect, but she must leave immediately if she were to arrive at Leo's castle before sundown, and the end of her month. Though it saddened her to part with her mother and Isaac once more, she remembered the look in Leo's eyes when he had asked her to return. Her will pulled her two ways, but it was not against returning, and so she saddled her horse, packed her small bag, and set off.

On the road between the farm and the Lady's house, a grey shire horse came galloping towards her.

'Issy! Issy! I have found the door!' Isaac's face was flushed with excitement. 'There is a small door in the cellar, and the key fits. Have you time to open it with me?'

Though desperate to be part of this adventure with him, Issy had already stretched her month to the very limit.

'I already have a hard ride ahead,' she said. 'But dream of me tonight, Isaac, and tell me everything.'

Isaac's face fell, but he squeezed her hand to show that he understood.

'Take my horse, at least,' he said. 'She is faster than the one you ride.'

They shared one final embrace, and Isobel rode off alone.

When she reached the castle, Leo was not waiting to greet her.

'Leo!' she called in the high-ceilinged entrance hall. 'Leo!'

She rushed from room to room. Was she too late? Had something happened because of her broken promise?

Just as her fear began to transform into panic, she heard a soft, growling voice.

'Issy.'

She flung open the nearest door and saw him, collapsed on the floor, his mane limp and greying, his eyes dull.

'Leo, darling.'

She hurried over to kneel at his side, and lifted his head into her lap.

'Issy,' he growled. 'You came back.'

'As I said I would.'

'You came freely, and left freely, and returned freely?'

'Of course I did,' said she. 'Who could have made me come back?'

She blinked the tears from her eyes, and when they were clear Leo no longer looked like Leo.

A young man lay across her lap. His hair was golden, his face smooth and clean shaven, his eyes dark and finely proportioned, his mouth handsome.

Isobel slid him away from her and stood up. The man smiled up at her. It was not the oddly drooping smile she knew. It was the smile of a thousand other young men.

'Leo?' she asked warily.

The young man sat up.

'You have saved me,' he said.

'I have?'

'You came to me, even in my beastly form, and stayed because you wanted to. You returned to me, though a beast I was still, because you cared for me. And by doing so, you have freed me of the beast forever. This,' he touched his pale, furless cheeks, 'is my true self. I am a Prince, though I could not tell you before.'

He brought himself up onto one knee before Isobel.

'And now,' he said, 'for all you have done, for all the feelings we have nurtured together, there is one thing I can give you in return. We shall be married.'

Isobel waited, but he did not say what she wanted him to say. She answered anyway.

'And if I do not desire it?'

Prince Leonardo only laughed. He stood and took her hands.

'We shall hold a feast to celebrate our engagement.'

Isobel's heart quivered.

'And if I do not desire it?'

He pulled her closer.

'We shall have all the nobles of the land to our wedding.'

Isobel's blood began to thrum in her ears.

'And if I do not desire it?'

The Prince held her.

'And for now, I shall kiss you.'

Isobel waited for what she knew was not coming.

'And if I do not desire it?'

'I love you, Belle.'

Isobel thrust her palms hard against his chest, sending the Prince staggering backwards.

'Belle!' he cried. 'What is the matter? We have shared so much over these past months. Has all your affection vanished?'

'My affection is as it always was,' said Isobel, refusing the tears that threatened to pour. 'But it seems that the man I fell in love with has disappeared.'

'I am here, dear Belle. Are you not pleased by the beauty within the beast?'

'My Leo was never a beast,' she said. 'He was a gentleman. And he knew my name.'

And she took the horse Issy back into the night, leaving the Prince Leonardo with his castle and his wealth and his beauty.

*

Isaac was unable to sleep. He dozed off several times into the place where he met Isobel, but she was never there and he found himself waking suddenly after he had waited there for a few minutes.

And every so often the door would creep into his mind.

Without Isobel at his side he had not had the confidence to open it. What on earth could the Lady be hiding, after all? He was sure it was nothing good.

In the dark hours of the early morning, eyes puffy from lack of sleep, Isaac was unable to bear it any longer. He took the ring of keys and a small oil lamp and, in his nightshirt and bare feet, went down to the cellar.

The lock was old and stiff. It took some effort to turn the key, and when he managed it the bolt slid open with a clunk that echoed through the empty cellar. He pushed open the wooden door and had to stoop to pass under the low frame. Inside he could smell something heavy and rusty and thick, something that seemed to have congealed in the air. When he moved his feet, they felt like they were pulling away from something sticky. He raised the lamp and let its light show him the small room.

Blood covered the floor and walls.

Standing to attention, eyes wide and glassy, stitches up the abdomen showing where they had been cut open and stuffed with preservatives, were the bodies of six men.

The shock of it threw Isaac back against the wall, from which he threw himself when he felt the cold, sour blood seeping quickly through his nightshirt. He cried aloud, dropped the lamp, and clawed his way through empty air to the door. He twisted the key that was still in the lock, shutting away the horror once more. Up the cellar steps he stumbled, and once above ground he saw, in the moonlight that streamed through the windows, that his hands, his arms, his feet, were all sticky and red.

His heart all but stopped when he heard a sound at the front door.

'My, my,' said Lady Gormain, removing her hat and coat and shaking her head at him. 'I see you are not as honest as you pretend to be.'

Isaac backed away.

'Why are you covered in blood, young man?' she asked.

He shook his head, his tongue held with terror.

'What have you seen?' she asked.

Isaac could not stop his eyes flickering towards the door to the cellar.

'I am not best pleased with you,' she said, and from her tall riding boot she pulled a long, thin blade. She raised it high, and Isaac froze.

'No,' said a firm voice from behind her. 'I have lost my Leo today, and I will be damned if I will lose my brother too.'

The Lady, stunned by the sudden voice, made a half-turn behind her. Her grip loosened as she did, and Issy pulled the blade from her grasp and slid it across Lady Gormain's throat.

## TIME OUT O' MIND

On the very Edge of Life and the very Edge of Death, the Ferrier waits alone. There is a world behind her, a world of children born, adults wed, wars waged, cities spread. There is a world ahead of her, a world of tranquillity and reunited loved ones, a world of peace for those who do not drown along the way.

Yet neither world is hers, for there must be one to take the best across the river to their next existence, to tip the worst over the side of her little wooden boat, and to let the rest try themselves on the journey.

It is a lonely life. The worst on the boat scare her. The best on the boat only stare eagerly at the shore, desperate to see again their departed. The rest pace to and fro, rocking the boat and muttering to themselves, until the Ferrier has heard enough to choose whether they will drown or cross.

Somewhen in the eternity of the Edge, from the world behind her, a man emerges. He is tall and dark with tightly curled hair and a small beard on his chin and around his mouth. Though his body has been healed by his passing through the veil, his clothes are still torn and the fabric still tinted with blood.

The man looks about himself, confused as they always are. He cannot remember what has happened to him.

'This is the Edge, and I am the Ferrier,' she tells him, as she always tells them. 'You are dead.'

'Dead?' he asks.

'Quite dead.'

He looks at his healthy body, but sees the damage to his clothes.

'How?'

'You were standing by the side of a road with your wife. You were being extra cautious, but somebody else was not. There was alcohol in her blood, and she did not drive as she normally would. You pushed your wife aside, but you were hit. Your body was dragged across the ground, grazing your arms and legs. Your organs were severely damaged by the impact. You died at the scene.'

The man looks at his hand, at his knees, at his chest. He touches himself as though he expects to find tender flesh, broken ribs, open wounds. The Ferrier waits, for she is used to people taking their time to absorb their own death. It does not bother her. She has all the time beyond the world.

'And my wife?' he asks her, when he has found his body to be whole and without pain.

'A sprained ankle. Nothing more.'

'The baby?'

'Too small in her womb to be affected. The fluid around it absorbed the shock of the fall. It likely noticed nothing.'

'Then all is well,' says the man, and he steps onto the boat and sets his eyes on the shore of the other world.

The Ferrier watches his face as she pushes the boat from the shore. His smile is quite clam, his eyes hold no fear, and he looks so pretty sitting there in her boat. She does not speak to passengers. It is not her way. Since the human race gave itself souls, she has been ferrying them silently across this endless lake, and yet in all that time only a handful have said a word to her once they set foot on the boat. Of those handful, not one conversation has been started by the Ferrier herself.

And yet this pretty man in her boat, who looks more peaceful than any soul she has seen before, makes her want like she has never wanted before to have more than the silent, lonely existence with her boat and her lake.

'Who will you see again?' she asks the man, wondering if there are already shadows gathering at the far shore for him.

'I don't know,' he says. 'My parents are alive. Perhaps my grandparents, though I never knew them in life. No friend or cousin or sibling of mine has ever died. So yes, my ancestors, should they wish to know me, may be waiting. But this will be a beginning for me, not a reunion.'

He does not look sad to think of his lonely new world, one full of strangers in which he must wait for his wife while wishing that her life would never end. The Ferrier finds this strange, for her world is one of strangers and it is such a cold way to live.

'You do not have to reach the shore,' she tells the man.

'I don't?'

'You don't. Some people are tipped in the middle you know, and eternally drown in this lake.'

The man chuckles, which she is not expecting.

'I think I'll take the shore over another endless death, Madam Ferrier.'

'I did not mean that for you,' she says. 'There is another option.'

'There is?' Though the man sounds mildly interested, his eyes are still on the shore, which draws closer with every push of the Ferrier's pole. 'And what is that?'

'You could ferry with me,' she says. 'If you stay on this boat with me, you would have a companion to talk to until your wife passes through the veil.'

'And what then?'

The Ferrier pauses in her punting and lets the boat bob in place.

'You are thinking that I want to trap you,' she says.

'There are stories of ferrymen trying to take the place of dead souls in paradise.'

'You will only take my place if you ferry yourself. If you only sit in my boat as a passenger, then you will be able to change your mind and step out onto the shore whenever you wish. In a day, a week, months, years. It doesn't matter how long your ferry journey takes.'

The man turns on the bench and looks up at the Ferrier, and in his eyes she sees pity.

'Could I not step onto the shore and still visit you when you bring other souls across?'

The Ferrier shakes her head.

'Once you step onto the shore, I cannot see you.'

The man frowns, looks to the shore and back to the Ferrier.

'You cannot see all those people over there? Lined up along the bank, waiting for us?'

The Ferrier stares at the empty shore, shrouded in mist and barren to her gaze. She shakes her head.

'My world is the Edge,' she tells him. 'I am neither one nor the other.'

'I am sorry, Ferrier,' and he looks it, and she knows he is. 'I cannot stay with you. I am not for the Edge, I am for the other world.' He turns back to the shore, where he can see faces he knows from photographs. 'Though the ones I love are still in the living world, there are ones over there who can share stories of them. My wife's father died before I could meet him, and he can tell me of my wife before I met her. My grandparents are there, who can tell me of my parents before I was born. There is too much there for me, Ferrier.'

The Ferrier holds her pole tightly in both hands, squeezing hard against the sorrow in her heart.

The boat sways as the man stands up, reaches for the Ferrier, and lays his hands upon her shoulders.

'There is always hope,' he tells her. 'You may find someone one day. Perhaps even my wife. Maybe when her time comes she will wish to stay here, between me and our living child, until we can all be united as a family. Perhaps she can be your companion.'

The Ferrier sighs, her hands relax, and she begins once more to push the boat towards the empty shore.

Before the man steps out to greet his ancestors, he turns back to the Ferrier with one last smile.

'Thank you, Ferrier,' he says. 'Good luck.'

And then he steps, and as soon as his foot touches the sand he vanishes from her world, never to be seen again.

*

The Ferrier does not feel time. She is endless and ancient, and time for her would be of no use. She has no days and nights in her world, just an existence that stretches into eternity. People pass through the veil one by one, and she ferries them one by one, and so many thousands of millions of souls journey on her boat that time would make it impossible for her to do her job.

Therefore she cannot know that seven months have passed in the living world when a woman arrives through the veil. She is small and dark and has shining black hair cut off at her chin. Her face is round, the outer corners of her eyes are high and her lips are smiling even though she does not know what is happening.

'Hi, babe,' she says to the Ferrier, and the Ferrier does not know what to say. She has never been addressed as a friend like this. She remembers a soul she ferried who looked at her with sorrow in his pretty eyes, and she is drawn to the woman.

'This is the Edge, and I am the Ferrier. You are dead.'

'Fair enough. It was the little one, I guess?'

The Ferrier's passengers are normally confused. She has not met anyone who has guessed their own death.

'You were giving birth, but it – '

'I don't need to know the ins and outs,' says the woman with a wave of her hand. 'Do you know if my baby is okay?'

'The baby is alive and healthy.'

'I was going to call her Fang. My mum and in-laws know, so hopefully they'll do that. It means fragrant. She's a flowery, perfumed baby.' The woman laughs happily at the thought of the daughter she will never know. 'I hope she has a good life. That's all we can hope, isn't it, for our babies?'

Without being told, she steps into the Ferrier's boat. The Ferrier starts to punt.

'Am I going up or down, then?' the woman asks.

'There is no up or down. There is drowning, or there is the shore. You are going to the shore.'

'That's nice. Or is it? It can't be worse than drowning.'

'The shore is good,' the Ferrier assures her.

The boat cuts neatly through the smooth water and the woman dangles a hand over the edge of the boat.

'If I go for a swim, will I drown?' she asks.

'This is not a lake for swimming,' says the Ferrier. 'Once you set foot on the shore, this lake will be gone and the water you see here will be safe.'

'I'll wait then.'

The Ferrier remembers what the pretty man said about his wife, and as she thinks and watches this beautiful, carefree woman humming to herself in the boat, she slows. The boat comes to a halt. The woman looks up.

'We're not at the shore yet.'

'No,' says the Ferrier. 'I thought I should let you know that you don't have to go.'

'But I don't want to drown.'

'Once you are on the shore, the Edge will be lost to you, and you will be as far as you can be from the living world. If you wanted, you could stay on the Edge, closer to your daughter.'

Tears spill down the woman's cheeks, but she is still smiling.

'But I wouldn't be with her, would I? So there's no point. My dad is over there, on the shore. And my husband. Unless they drowned, of course.'

She stands up in the boat, holds a hand above her eyes like a sailor looking out for land.

'I think I see them,' she says.

'You would go to them one day. If you stay here with me, one day your daughter will come through the veil, and I can take you together to your husband, her father, and you can all be together again. You wouldn't be here for ever.'

But the woman shakes her head.

'You're lonely here, aren't you? But I can't be the one to help you. I'd only resent you, knowing my husband was waiting and I was keeping myself away from him. We will wait together for our daughter.'

So the Ferrier takes the woman to the shore, and watches her face grow more excited the closer they come, and sees her wave and shout out. But still, before she touches the sand, the woman with the silken hair and exquisite eyes turns and hugs the Ferrier tightly.

'I'm sorry that this sucks for you. But I love my dad too much, and my husband. I need to go to them. Don't lose hope, though. Think about my daughter. She will never know her parents, and maybe if all her friends and lovers outlive her she will wait here with you for them.'

She leaps from the boat, and the Ferrier does not get to see her throw herself into her father's arms, release him to kiss her lover, and go arm in arm with them into her death.

*

The souls are endless, a constant stream of confused, scared, lost, hopeful, angry things that are too distracted by their own demise to have any time for the Ferrier, even here in her timeless realm. She ferries on, as she has always done, as decades pass in the world behind her. No one touches her heart, no one speaks to her of her, only of themselves, of those ahead of them, of those behind them.

The Ferrier often sees a curl, an iris, a tooth, any number of little things that remind her of the man with pitying eyes or the woman whose smile never dropped.

Too many souls to count have passed her before she sees the one that must be theirs. She has the soft round face of her mother. Her eyes too are shaped like her mother's and hold the depth of feeling that her father's did. He has given her hair thick curls and her body more thickness and height that her mother had.

'I'm dead, aren't I?'

There is the confidence of her mother and the calm of her father.

'This is the Edge, and I am the Ferrier. You are dead.'

She is very young to be dead. A woman in her middle years, in the very prime of her life. There are crinkles of laughter around her eyes and mouth which deepen as she smiles at the Ferrier.

'Hi, Ferrier. I'm Fang. Where are you sailing today?'

The Ferrier waves a hand to the distant shore that she cannot see.

'Where I always sail,' she says.

'May I come with you?' asks Fang.

The Ferrier is taken aback. No one has ever asked her permission to step into the boat. It is what her boat is for.

'My duty is to ferry you to the otherworld, where the souls of everyone you have ever lost will be waiting for you.'

'And what if I have lost no-one?' Fang asks, making no move towards the boat.

The Ferrier does not know why she has asked this, for she knows full well that Fang has lost both parents and that they will be eager to meet her.

'Your mother and father are waiting,' she tells her. 'Do you not want to meet them?'

Fang looks back over her shoulder, back to the veil she has passed through, as though she might catch a glimpse of what she has left.

'It's funny,' she says, looking back to the Ferrier. 'Dad died before I was born, and Mum died giving birth to me. But I feel like I know them already. I have other family,' and she waves towards the veil, for they are all still in the world of the living, 'and they've told me so much about them for as long as I can remember. I dream about them, and they talk to me. Sometimes I'm sad that I never met them, but sometimes I see a picture of them and feel like I can remember them.'

'Then now is the time to meet them,' says the Ferrier.

'I suppose so.'

Fang finally steps into the boat, and the Ferrier pushes it out into the lake.

She feels something she has never felt before. Though the Ferrier has never failed in her purpose, she has never felt satisfied. She has existed, she has done what she is there to do, and that is all. But she has thought often of Fang's parents, the only two souls to have ever moved her heart, and now to be ferrying their daughter to them feels good and right.

Half way across the lake, Fang lays a hand on the Ferrier's arm and stops her punting.

'What else can happen, Ferrier?' she asks.

The Ferrier points down into the deep, dark water beneath them.

'The bad ones are tipped overboard,' she says. 'The good ones are taken to the shore. Those are the two things that can happen.'

'And what about you, Ferrier?'

'Me?'

'You.'

The Ferrier sits. She has never sat in her boat with a passenger before. Sometimes, when she returns from the shore of the otherworld, she might sit in her boat for a moment before another comes through the veil, but the flow of souls is constant. She looks out over the lake, at the infinite water on which she lives.

'I am here. I am always here.'

'Why?'

'Why? There is no why. I am the Ferrier. I am on the Edge. Someone has to be.'

Fang's hand is still on the Ferrier's arm.

'Must that someone be alone?'

The empathy of her father is in her eyes, the warmth of her mother in the arms she wraps around the Ferrier.

'I remember your parents,' she says.

'Do you remember all the souls you ferry?'

The Ferrier shakes her head.

'I remembered none until your father. He told me of your mother, and when she came I knew. She told me of you, and when you came...'

The Ferrier's eyes fill. She is timeless, ageless, endless, and yet this is the first time she has cried. She has had no use for tears before.

'Your parents are good. The very best. My heart beat for them, in a way it had never beaten before. You will know such joy when you see them, I am sure.'

Fang holds the Ferrier. She lets the salty tears dampen her shoulder. She feels the sobs rock the little vessel. She holds her head up and squints to the shore, where she can see two figures standing, hand in hand.

'A part of me has always wanted to meet them,' she tells the Ferrier. 'But my life hasn't been empty without them. I can wait.'

The Ferrier dries her face.

'Wait for what?' she asks.

'I am not ready to be pulled so far away from my living ones. I have grandparents who raised me. I have lifelong friends. I know I can't get back to them, I know I can't see them, but I feel closer to them here. If I touch the shore, I'll feel too far away. Can I stay with you, Ferrier? Can I stay on this boat, on this lake, on the Edge with you?'

The Ferrier feels an ache deep inside her chest, as though something is straining with a pressure that must be relieved.

Fang's hands clasp over the Ferrier's.

'Please?'

*

'This is the Edge, and we are the Ferriers. You are dead.'

It will not last for ever, the Ferrier knows. Eventually a soul Fang knows will come through the veil, and the Ferrier will take them both to the shore, leave the woman who has filled her heart, and be alone once more. But for now she is happy to ferry the souls as she has always done, and to drift slowly back to the veil with Fang's head in her lap, hands entwined, enjoying the endless lack of time for however long it might last.

## OF DREAMS AND LIES

Look at her, the perfect brat, as she whirls from man to man, tossing her golden curls, blinking her cobalt orbs, moistening her cherry lips deliberately slowly with her pointed pink petal of a tongue. The secret to her wealth, you ask? She will giggle, a sound of sweet girlish innocence that never fails to fool, and tell you: straw. And she will with one finger stroke the fine thread of gold that trickles down from her neck and nestles itself between her silicone breasts. She will watch your eyes watching her finger, drawn irresistibly downwards. If you are not handsome enough for her she will scold your ogling, perhaps dole out a slap if she is feeling particularly lonesome and needy, and the paparazzi will flock to her defence, splashing pictures of the perverted fiend across the tabloids' front pages and praising our beloved Golden Treasure, ever the tragic victim, for soldiering on despite the trauma like the little trouper that she is.

But the secret, you ask, the real secret? Perhaps if enough champagne has been drizzled down her gullet, if you have pounded her hard enough, if she has not yet tossed you aside, if she is resting on your warm, damp chest in the afterglow, her lips might skip their way up your shoulder, neck, cheek, and nibble on your ear and she may tell you:

'I spin straw into gold.'

It is a rare antique that she sits by, her hand wrapped around a spoke of the wheel, idly spinning it back and forth. When she sees me she smiles, a cartoon star of light pinging off her tic tac teeth, and heartily thrusts the wheel into a spin it is too delicate for. Her smile ceases the instant I slap her filthy hands away from the precious thing. The eyes she always tries to keep so wide and pure are suddenly foul cuts of fury, her lips like satiated leeches contorted around her snarling gnashers as she hisses at me: I will never, *ever*, touch her again.

But for a decade I have toed the line, never challenging, always serving, waiting and waiting for the day that she will finally give me what she promised. And so I demand of her: or else what?

Or else, and I can see the wicked gleam of delighted triumph in her cold, cruel eyes as she tells me, she might want to take a little trip to see her doctor. And we both know what that means, don't we? The contract still stands. I will only get my payment, when it finally arrives, if I have kept my end of the bargain. I must keep spinning.

She keeps me spinning for months on end, night after night, teasing out the stiff rods from the bales she has surrounded me with, ever so gently, the wheel ever turning, the shimmering thread entwining the reel until it can hold no more. My eyes grow red, sore and tired, aching in my poorly lit cell of a room. So close now, so close, so very nearly free...

I hear groans from downstairs, but I must keep spinning. I hear her pacing, moaning, panting, wailing. I hear the midwife crooning to her, calming her, helping her: push now, keep pushing, she can see the crown.

Like a blow to the ear, my baby's first choke of a cry hammers its way into my head. Momentum keeps the wheel whizzing around for another circuit as my hands are released and I abandon my post. I am off the stool, across the bare boarded floor, out of the door, down the winding staircase, following the sound of the little howling infant downstairs – a boy or a girl? I am its mother and I do not yet know. I cannot bear not knowing. So close, so close. There is the door to the bedroom where my little one waits for me, and it is opening for me as I tear down the hallway. Surely the infant feels how cold the touch of gold is, knows deep down that the woman that birthed it is not its mother, is waiting, without realising it, for me, the one who will love it and nurture it and –

A cry from the doorway: That's the one.

Me? I'm the one? The one what? My path is suddenly blocked by a hulking figure in black, and I hear the whimper of my new-born and all I want is – Come where? A huge hammy hand clamps onto my upper arm and tries to force me away from the room, but that tiny little sob is breaking my heart and I must see – What's happening? But the Golden Treasure won't tell me. In her arms is a bundle, my bundle, but it is wrapped too well, too tightly, too safe, and I cannot see a porcelain hand, a tuft of hair, a marble eye. She squeezes the bundle tighter against her Barbie breast, but the embrace is full of spite not warmth and I see that glint in her eye as she points dramatically at me and wails: I threatened to take her baby, I was blackmailing her, I said I'd *kill* the baby.

No, where are you taking me? But I haven't seen my baby, my baby, give me my baby! You promised! You gave me your word! That baby is mine!

As I am dragged backwards away from my promised one, the Golden Treasure sticks out her index finger and lowers it – slowly, slowly – towards the bundle, and my heart skips. His hand, her hand, my baby's hand, will surely reach up and grab. I will catch just that one glimpse of my child before they take me away, and that will be enough, anything will be enough, even the tip of a fresh pink toe would be enough. Her finger moves closer, I am hauled further, so close, so far, so close, so far...

I am gone too soon.

## ATHWART MEN'S NOSES

The Princess doesn't want a Prince, she wants a plaything. Something to use and abuse, to throw away into the gutter when she's had her fill and to watch, if it pleases her to do so, as it crawls its way back to her, battered and bruised, whimpering and sobbing, begging for more. She will pluck her plaything from the dance floor tonight, rip his roots from the ground and pot him instead in her chambers where he will grow and thrive, or wither and die. She smiles to herself as her maids encircle her lithe body with stiff cotton drill and whalebone. She does not wince as the foot is pressed into her back and the cords are drawn to bind her. She raises her arms and lets them slip the silk over her head. It falls gently over her painfully forced curves, floating over her hips and cascading to the floor, the fabric so light she barely feels it covering her.

She dismisses the maids before she adds her final touch. She glides towards the boiled-sweet panes of her stained windows, pushes them open, leans out and with a tiny gold knife cuts free one flower from the bed beneath the sill. She tucks the stem between her breasts and allows the head to poke over the neck of her dress, inviting visitors to come closer to the delicate thing. As she does so, a single, clear bead of moisture drops like a tear from the pointed end of the largest petal of the perfectly colourless lily.

*

She sits high upon her crystal seat with the delicate tip of her chin barely resting on the snowy white softness of her gently curled fingers. She reaches up the other hand and moves the pearl that hangs around her neck a fraction of an inch with one talon, then replaces the hand without a sound on the arm of her throne. She surveys the scene before her: every young man of the land is here, from the sixteen year old son of the seamstress to the duke's heir with thirty-one years under his belt. She is to choose tonight, so the invitations claimed, a husband. She has her pick of all the young men on offer, and yet she remains unsatisfied. She has had suitors before, many an experienced lad with a wooing technique to rival Casanova's, and with them she would amuse herself until the boredom and monotony of them set in and she would be forced to cast them aside in search of another. And yet, despite the trail of discarded lovers that litters the path behind her, never has she found a man to truly satisfy her desires. So here she sits, her eyes roaming the floor for that one male with the elusive spark she has not yet found.

And there he is.

He stands awkwardly in the corner of the hall. He is holding in his hand a glass of champagne, something he has never done before. He is trying to look moody and mysterious, but instead only looks vulnerable and alone. The Princess leans forwards, both hands now grasping the arms of the throne. She has to bite down on her tongue to stop it flicking out and licking her plump red lips in anticipation. She rises gracefully and descends the stairs to the dance floor. She floats across to the corner in which the hapless young boy hides and extends to him her elegant hand. His face is the very picture of awe as he gazes on her as though she were an angel released from Heaven, and he trips clumsily as she leads him to the centre of the room to dance. As he does so, she glances down disdainfully and sees that his shoes, though beautifully made in midnight blue silk with polished silver buckles, are not well fitted. He has borrowed them for the night in an attempt to impress her. She finds herself letting out a scornful laugh as he blushes and stuffs his feet back into the slippers, but it does not matter that he hears, for she is the Princess and can do what she likes.

She dances with this fragile ornament of a boy all evening, admiring all the while the beauty of his young face, the soft curls of the startlingly blond hair that is tied at his nape with a fine silk ribbon, the smooth touch of those hands that have never dreamed of being in the places frequented by the hands of the Men in the room. She does not take her eyes off him for a moment.

It is seven dances before she has feasted on his frail beauty for long enough. When the seventh dance has finished, she drops her hand from his shoulder and is amused to see in his eyes a flicker of despair; he thinks she is leaving him. Just to taunt him, she releases his hand from her grasp as well, turns on her heel and marches haughtily away from him. In the great glass mirror of the wall, she sees the shame, the disappointment, even the beginnings of humiliated tears pricking at the corners of his big blue eyes. Oh, what a sweet, naive little boy he is. She spins back around and demands of him,

'Well?'

He is confused, taken aback, unsure of how he is supposed to respond to a meaningless demand spoken with such arrogant rudeness.

'Are you coming with me or not?'

And there again is that adorable face of wonderment as he stares at her. He scurries after her as she breezes out of the room. She leads him down the long hallway, carpeted with deep crimson, and into the huge entrance hall with its marvellous sculptures of polished marble. He trails after her as she ascends the great stairs, her hand hovering above the golden stair chord and her feet seeming never to touch the ground. She can feel now his youthful mix of trepidation and anticipation, can smell it in the fresh sweat beneath his cheap perfume, and silently dares him to speak – how she would love to hear that barely-broken voice, to cut it off with her sharp tongue and see how much he will love her to shame him – but he does not. She hears him trip again in his too-big shoes and again lets him hear the music of her derisive laugh. As they approach a bend in the corridor, she does not turn but instead continues directly forward, not faltering in her stride, towards the pale sheen of an expensive, heavy tapestry that hangs upon the stone wall. She enjoys the boy's gasp as she, not dropping her speed even a fraction, appears to be heading straight into the hard, grey stone. But she does not slam into the wall, as he expects, and instead disappears through the tapestry. She would like to stop and observe his reaction, drinking in every sugary drop of his innocent marvelling, but she cannot do that; she must retain the mood she has created. Her fun will come later and she is happy to wait. She hears him push his way through the light drapery that covers the entrance of this passage and the illusion is broken. The first spindly thread of his innocent trust had been snipped. Before he leaves the palace, she will have hacked away at several more.

He follows her down this hidden corridor, his footfalls tentative, as it winds its way through the thick walls of the castle, gradually gaining height as they are sucked deeper and deeper down its flame lit length.

Finally, the passage spits the young one out into a large, cold chamber where the Princess is waiting. She is smiling at him, a gesture which he politely attempts to return but does not fully understand. She slowly raises her hands to her head and entwines them in her golden hair, raising it up to reveal the gentle curves of her shoulders and smooth hollows of her collarbones. She turns to reveal the back she has exposed.

'Release me,' she commands.

The boy does not understand. Oh, sweet virginity! He steps forwards cautiously, worried that he will appear stupid to this creature of Heaven.

'Undo my buttons,' she says.

The boy is startled, but who is he to disobey the Princess? He, a lowly merchant's son? He raises shaking fingers to the pearl buttons that fasten the back of her dress and slowly slips the first one from its silver loop. He hesitates.

'What's the matter? Are you scared?' the Princess taunts. 'Oh, had I known you were such a coward I would have chosen a Man for my dance partner, not a boy.'

'I am not scared, my Lady,' the boy insists, though his fear is so intense she can all but see it radiating from his fragile form. The boy lifts his hands once more and continues his task, his nimble fingers working quickly despite their trembling. The silk slips over the corset beneath and cascades to the floor as the Princess releases the cloud of gold hair from her fingers.

'Ahhh,' she sighs. She turns slowly back to the boy, drinking in every drop of his terror as he struggles to keep his eyes on her face. His cheeks have flushed a most glorious shade of pink and his eyes have begun to water just a little as they strain to stay looking upwards. 'Will you not look at me?' she asks. 'Am I not beautiful enough for you?'

'You are magnificent, my Lady,' the boy stutters, 'but I cannot defile you with my unworthy eyes.'

She laughs and shakes out her mane.

'Then if you will not look at me, I have but one command for you, little one,' she says with a smile. 'And this you must do, for I am your Princess and you must serve me.'

'Of course, my Lady,' says the boy and, as she knew he would, he cannot help but make the customary bow. His eyes catch a glimpse of the body they have been trying so desperately to avoid, and their warm blue gaze is captivated. He is powerless to do anything but stare at the long, lean legs coated with their dusting of white stocking, the tiny pinched-in waist held tightly by rigid bones, the uplifted breasts that heave over the top of the corset at each breath the Princess takes. And still there on her bosom is the lily.

'Take the flower,' she says. 'If you succeed in plucking the flower without touching my skin, I will let you go. If you cannot, you are mine.'

The boy steps forwards, his hand outstretched towards the snowy petals. He knows before he tries that he already belongs to her.

*

The Princess settles herself regally upon her throne once more for the closing ceremony. Her father makes a speech while holding her bony white hand in his large, sweaty, red one. He pats her wrist with his inflated fingers and booms heartily to the crowd while she stands perfectly still, his little ornament, with her eyes fixed upon the pitiful figure of the boy. His left stocking sags a little at the ankle where he has not pulled it up properly; his breeches are a little askew at the knee; a button is missing from his waistcoat, an imperfection which could easily have been hidden by smartly fastening the frock coat he wears had he sense enough left to think of such a thing. She curtseys to the crowd, her eyes still locked upon those of the boy, and she blows to him a delicate kiss that the crowd believes is for all. The boy is the first to hurry out of the ballroom.

*

It is in the early hours of the next morning that the Princess takes a stroll around the gardens, an exquisite shawl draped around her shoulders to shield her from the slight chill. She is thinking of the boy, of how young he is and how little he knows, and she is wondering to herself if he has been changed now. The thought begins to worry her, for no other boy in the Kingdom, as far as she knows, possesses that rare charm of innocence. She needs that charm to keep her satisfied. But perhaps this can never be, for once she has toyed with a naive one she has altered him and stolen from him the very essence that makes him so perfectly beautiful to her. She wonders if the boy she danced with is gone forever.

And then she sees the shoe. Abandoned on the palace steps, it is silky and midnight blue with a polished silver buckle. It is left as though the wearer, in a hurry in his badly fitting shoes, had simply stepped right out of it and, with the innocent panic of a child, run blindly on without. The Princess bends to retrieve it and, with the delighted giggle of a maiden, picks up her skirts and rushes to find her father.

*

The boy waits nervously at home. He is waiting for the Princess. He knows she will arrive eventually. He does not want her to. So many young men have been eagerly searching their wardrobes for shoes matching the description and throwing out one of the pair in hope of convincing the Princess that he is the one, and yet here sits the boy with a feeling of despair growing ever stronger in his gut as he stares helplessly at the shoe he still possesses.

His father is proud and says he must have made a 'real impression'. He digs the boy in the ribs with a plump elbow and gives a vulgarly exaggerated wink as he says it.

His mother dabs her eyes with a dish cloth and wails incoherently about her little boy growing up and flying the nest.

The boy says nothing. He simply stares and stares at the shoe, his mind having flown from his small family home to the cavernous room within the stone walls of the Princess's lair. This is his fate and he cannot escape it. After all, who is he to refuse a proposal from the Princess?

There is a knock at the door, a knock that would sound snooty if knocks could sound so, followed by a loud announcement that the knocker is of the King's Court and accompanied by the Princess. The boy rises slowly from his seat as his father hurries to the door to greet the royal guest. As he catches his first glimpse of the hem of the Princess's dress, he sinks into a low bow and greets her with the customary acknowledgement. Though his eyes remain on the bare boards of the floor directly in front of his toes, he can feel the Princess advancing on him. He feels her reach out her arm and lay her palm on his soft, fair curls with all the gentle love of a Goddess.

'You may rise, little one.'

He does so, albeit reluctantly, and finds himself drawn irresistibly to the lily she is wearing once again. He wants her to give him permission for a second time, to command him to take the flower from her and to pull the cords of her corset loose again and to force him to stay still while she rips the shirt from his back.

'The shoe. Put it on.'

He drops his gaze a little to the hand on which the shoe is perched. He watches her kneel before him and raise his bare foot with a feather-light touch of her fingertips. She slips the shoe on. His parents hold their breath. The Princess claps her hands with glee.

'Oh! The only boy in the Kingdom with feet so small and precious that they do not fill the shoe!'

'Yes, my Lady,' the boy whispers, and he places the second shoe on the floor and steps into it.

The Princess stares at his feet for a moment and, with her plump, smiling lips, she plants a single kiss on his left ankle.

'You are mine now, little one,' she says.

*

The Princess did not find a Prince, she found a plaything. She found something to use and abuse, to throw away into the gutter when she's had her fill and to watch, since it pleases her to do so, as he crawls his way back to her, as he always does, battered and bruised, whimpering and sobbing, begging for more for ever after.

## CHILDREN OF AN IDLE BRAIN

There once was a girl whose head was full of stories. When she was very little, she went out into her garden and saw another little girl sitting on the swing that hung from her apple tree. This little girl had curly brown hair and nutmeg skin and looked very much like the girl she saw every day in the mirror.

'Hello,' said the girl. 'Who are you?'

'I'm your sister, silly,' said the little girl on the swing. 'We're twins.'

The girl sat down on the swing next to her twin. They kicked their bare legs out together and flew up into the branches.

'I never knew I had a sister,' the little girl said.

'That's why I came to say hello,' said her twin.

When their father called them inside for dinner, the twins squeezed onto one chair and ate together from one plate. They bathed together that night and were tucked up side by side.

*

When the girl was not quite so little, when for a few years she and her twin had been sitting at the same desk at school and working in one notebook, they went out into their garden together. Snuggled down in the grass, almost completely hidden, they saw what look like a drawer handle. The girl looked harder and saw another just a couple of feet away. She took hold of one handle, her twin took hold of the other, and together they pulled up from the ground a flat window. Through the window came the sound of birds they had never heard in their garden, and the smell of warm rain and unfamiliar fruits.

121

'This must be a window to the jungle,' said the little girl.

Hand in hand with her twin, she stepped through to another world.

This world was very green and very damp and very colourful. In this world the girl and her twin met a jaguar and her cub. They learned a language of growls and purrs and followed this hunter from the soggy earth into the vast canopy. They learned how to sniff out food from a hundred miles away, to scrabble up trees and hang on to branches by the tips of their fingers. They learned what it is to be wild, to be buried deep in the green ferns and to sleep under the stars.

When their father called to them in the evening, they heard him even though he was on another continent. That night they hid beneath the same blanket, one hand each holding the same book, and read by torchlight.

The next day the girl and her twin chose another window, this time to an icy world of polar bears and frosty mermaids. They went to a desert land filled with tiny crabs, to a mountain range in search of yetis, to a cave of jewels where a dragon hid. The world kept turning, the girls kept exploring, and life was sweet.

*

When the girl was almost beyond little, it was harder and harder to ignore her twin in front of the other children at school. The girl sent her twin secret smiles, little gestures of their own language behind the backs of the other children, but they started to notice her looking constantly, longingly, at an empty space.

'It's time for me to go, isn't it?' said her twin to the girl one night as they sat on their bed with a book between them.

'No,' said the girl. 'Why should it be? You're my sister. I don't care if no-one else can see you.'

'But you will one day,' said her twin. She wiped a tear from her eye and let go of the book. 'I think it's better for me to go now, while you still love me.'

The girl thought about it, and felt the truth of what her twin said.

'You deserve more than to fade out of my life,' she told her twin.

'Thank you.'

One last time, they huddled up together beneath the blanket and shone their torch onto crisp old pages. One last time they dove into the story together, and when they reached the last word on the last page of the last chapter, the girl and her twin went hand in hand into the darkness of the garden. There were only the handles of one window this time. For a moment they clung to each other in silence, then they each tugged a handle. Through this window, they could see nothing. No trees, no sand, no stone. An unknown emptiness lay beyond.

Her twin squeezed her hand one last time and disappeared through the window. It snapped back to the ground as soon as she had passed through, and vanished.

'I suppose this is the end of stories and windows,' the girl said to herself, alone in a very ordinary garden.

She went to back bed.

*

When the girl was becoming a young lady, she sat in front of her Head Mistress.

'I hear you have been having trouble concentrating in your lessons,' said the Head Mistress.

'Have I? I hadn't noticed,' said the girl, not meaning to be cheeky. Her mind was on other things, on the book she had kept in her bag for years and returned to day after day.

'If things continue like this, it may have a serious effect on your *Future*, young lady. You need to start *Preparing*. It is high time you had a *Serious Think* about what you want to *Do* with your life, and began taking steps to achieve your *Goals*. You're an intelligent enough student, but you seem to lack *Direction*.'

The girl nodded blandly while the Head Mistress talked. When she was set free, she hurried along corridor after corridor until she found an empty classroom, and here she reached into her bag to retrieve her book. It was the same book she had shared with her twin on their last night together, a tale of a young man and his friend and their travels and misadventures.

'Goodness, she went on rather,' muttered the girl. She sat neatly on a chair, knees together and back straight, and opened her book near the beginning.

'What're you always studying for? You already know everything. Come on, have a drink, relax.'

'Some of us don't want to work in a coffee shop forever. Some of us want to do other things.'

'And that's lovely, but you're going to pass anyway. So. Are you coming tonight?'

'Absolutely not. Even if I didn't have this exam, why on earth would I want – '

The bell rang. The girl tightened her laces, rolled down the sleeves of her blouse, neatened her collar, and went to her next lesson. Under the desk, she opened the book again close to the middle.

'My hand! Take my hand!'

'Can't reach! I – I can't – '

'Swim for it! Come on, think of those pool races, all those summers! Don't give up on me now!

'Swim!'

'Excuse me?'

The girl looked up, rearranged her features to a less distressed expression, and scanned the board, the open text books of her classmates, anything that might give her a clue.

'The...rest of the potential survivors. Why didn't they just...swim?'

'If you'd been paying attention, you would have heard me say how the dinghy could only carry twelve and it took eleven days of sailing before they found land. Now, how could you expect the others to have swum that far?'

'They could have rotated. Twelve in the boat, the rest swimming. In shifts.'

Her teacher paused, his lips pursed and his brows angrily low.

'Let's all concentrate on the historical facts, and not fanciful ideas about what could have been.'

The girl tuned out her teacher's voice once more and felt the sudden, strong grip on her wrist. He'd made it.

\*

When the girl was nearing the end of her schooldays, she walked home from school with her tie loose, the sleeves of her blazer rolled up, hair undone. She stroked the spine of her book.

'Hot chocolate? I'll only charge you for a small.''

'Does your manager know you cheat the café out of money?'

'He knows it's only for you.'

She dipped her head and sped up, overtaking the father and child ahead of her.

'What's wrong?'

She stayed silent until she was crossing the empty park, not another soul in sight.

'Are you okay?'

She refocused her eyes and smiled across the counter at her favourite boy.

'Sure. Nothing's wrong. Marshmallows?'

Back at the girl's house, she shut herself up in her room. She rewound to when they were at school together and asked him for help with her homework.

> 'Since when did you care? I don't think I've seen you hand anything in all year.'

The girl laughed. There was a knock at her door.

'Are you on the phone? I thought you were working.'

'I am.'

'Good. I don't want another call from school. Don't let yourself slack off now. You've always worked so hard.'

The girl looked at the papers that covered her bedroom floor. There were notes, photocopies, practise papers, essays. There were draft applications to universities, letters about open days, booklets from campuses all over the country.

'Take my hand.'

> 'Help me.'

'I won't let us drown.'

\*

Far from home, the girl cups her hands around a cappuccino. Opposite her, her favourite boy has a hot chocolate with marshmallows and cream. The girl doesn't like coffee. As she thinks this, she senses something in the air. A ripple like they made with a skimmed stone on the gloriously blue lake they once found; or perhaps more like the heat haze that used to shiver above the grass in their school's grounds on those long days before the summer holidays. As the air trembles, the scene outside the window wavers, shifting in and out of focus. She blinks several times, waiting for the mirage to pass, then peers through the glass and sees the street that should be there. The illusion is over.

She runs a hand through her smooth black hair, scratches her cheek, thinks, 'I could do with a shave.'

39486285R00072

Printed in Poland
by Amazon Fulfillment
Poland Sp. z o.o., Wrocław